A

Paradise

Mark Tournoff

A Nightmare in Paradise

ISBN 0 9545072 0 7

Published by Forestdale Publications
70 Ladygrove
Pixton Way
Croydon
Surrey CR0 9LS

Design & production co-ordinated by:
The Better Book Company Ltd
Havant
Hampshire
PO9 2XH

Printed in England

Chapter 1

'Lucky' Hanson flicked a switch in the hallway and the gates to *Paradise* opened as if by magic. The path was clear for the majestic Ultramobile which was to convey them to the clinic. A second switch was pressed; a door in a row of seven garages opened and a gleaming red sports car trundled steadily forwards. The vehicle halted near the front door to the mansion as the garage door closed itself. This was 'Tuesday's car', as Hanson liked to call it, and it was his favourite. Today it was standing in for 'Thursday's car', which was (to its owner's displeasure) still undergoing repair work following the previous week's accident. A third switch ensured that all communications received in *Paradise* would be relayed directly to the Ultramobile.

As Hanson opened the front door his daughter Sophie came down the staircase. She had left it to the last moment to appear, as if to reinforce the message of disapproval at the purpose of the morning's journey. They walked silently to the limousine, which, sensing their presence, opened its doors to them, and closed them again once they were settled in their seats. Here on the estate the full range of the vehicle's automated features could be employed, but on the public roads outside of *Paradise* self-propelled vehicles were prohibited, so Hanson keyed in the password to put the sports car under his control.

An array of colourful digits on the dashboard presented him with diverse information: the temperature (20 degrees), the time (08:38), and the date (19:08:2009). They set off, and in an instant were through the gates, which obligingly closed behind them. The vehicle ran so smoothly and quietly that the sound of its engine was barely audible, even to its occupants. At length Lucky broke the silence:

'So have you thought any more about what I said last night?'

Sophie winced and shook her head, then replied:

'Dad, you know I don't agree with what you're doing. I'm not likely to have changed my mind overnight, am I?'

There was no response. She knew he was sulking, and felt a little guilty that she was the cause of his malaise. He was bound to keep trying to get her to reconsider. Nevertheless she was determined not to give in. In that respect, at least, they were alike.

'You don't give up easily, do you, Dad?' she observed eventually, smiling faintly as she glanced at him.

'Stubborn as a mule, as your mum used to say,' he acknowledged.

Sophie looked away, out of the passenger window at the hedgerows rushing by. Through the gaps she caught occasional glimpses of black and white, legs mainly, the odd head and neck, perhaps even a swishing tail. The Sussex air was fresh, and the atmosphere relaxed; it was not difficult to understand why one might want to remain there indefinitely. She put the seat back and looked up through the open roof. The azure sky was completely clear. True, there were little wisps of cloud resting on the tops of the hills, but the climbing sun had already left these behind; it was going to be a scorcher.

Sophie began to doze, but soon awoke to find that the sunlight was now flickering rapidly through thick treetops. It was as though they were travelling through a tunnel illuminated by strobe lighting. She realized they were in the Ashdown forest, and so must be nearly there. Soon they turned sharply left, onto a winding road that narrowed to become a single highway with passing places. Feeling increasingly uncomfortable with the speed at which they were travelling, Sophie protested:

'Dad, slow down! If there's anything coming towards you round one of these bends, you won't be able to stop.'

Her father grinned at her and said nothing. He enjoyed going a bit too fast, cutting corners, taking an unnecessary risk or two. It added excitement to the journey. The fact that he had come unstuck only the previous week did not deter him. There are people who refuse to learn their lessons in life, and Andrew Hanson was one of these people. If anything his daughter's remark enticed him to go faster. Indeed they almost overshot the turning for the clinic, which was marked by a large sign:

'PRIVATE ROAD: STRICTLY NO PUBLIC ACCESS'.

Sizeable speed humps forced Lucky to slow down. Two vehicles came past them from the opposite direction: the first was a long, shiny, black Mercedes with dark window glass: the second was a silver Ultramobile, with a young woman at the wheel. Lucky nodded and she smiled back at him.

'Do you know who that was?' he asked.

'No.'

'Tania Fenton.'

'The pop star?'

'Yes.'

They reached the security barrier. A man in a dark uniform greeted them politely, and checked their I D cards. He flashed a hand-held gadget along the length of the Ultramobile and examined the results briefly before inviting them to proceed.

'Those guards were armed,' Sophie observed.

'Well, the owner of the clinic and some of the surgeons have received death threats from those nutters campaigning against this. Amazing really…you would think they were trying to kill people, not make them live longer, wouldn't you?'

Sophie did not reply. She felt that the remark was aimed at her, although in fact her father was only giving voice to his thoughts.

They were halted by an immaculately dressed porter, who offered to park the Ultramobile. Lucky was quick to spot an opportunity to impress.

'It's okay, she can park herself.'

He waited in vain for an expression of surprise or a note of admiration. Self-propelled vehicles were not uncommon at the clinic, and the car park spaces were clearly numbered in order to accommodate them.

'Bay twelve is free, sir.'

Hanson keyed in the password and a digital face smiled at him through the centre of the steering wheel.

'Park in bay twelve,' Lucky commanded.

'Yes, Mr Hanson,' came the reply.

The Ultramobile waited until the Hansons were clear before setting off, then proceeded steadily to bay twelve. It reversed neatly into a position exactly in the centre of the bay. Lucky insisted on watching the vehicle complete its manoeuvre before allowing them to enter the clinic.

Chapter 2

Sophie checked her watch. It was midday, and they had been at the clinic for over two hours. On entering, they had been escorted to a large waiting room that was more reminiscent of a hotel lounge. They were served complimentary drinks, and Sophie was invited to peruse a list of facilities available to her while she waited for her father. These included a gym, a swimming pool and a library, all of which she declined in favour of a small room to herself. A massive TV screen offered her the choice of innumerable channels, an enormous range of films available on microdisk, or a wide selection of computer games. She opted instead to listen to some music, and from a panel in the arm of the chaise longue on which she was reclining selected her favourite string quartets. She could not tell exactly where the music was coming from, but the effect created by the system was that of being right in the middle of the four instrumentalists. She listened to Ravel, Debussy, Dvorak and Shostakovitch, and now started to feel restless, wishing to spend some time outside in the grounds under the blazing sun. Although Sophie felt hungry, she decided to resist the temptation of the lunch served free of charge at the clinic. Her father would be ready to leave in about an hour, and would be sure to want to visit a favourite pub they would pass on the return journey; she hoped he would agree to the minor detour she had in mind.

She pressed a buzzer and an attendant was with her in seconds.

'Would it be okay to take a stroll around the grounds?' Sophie asked.

'Most certainly, Miss Hanson,' the young man replied. 'Follow me, please.'

A great deal of thought and care had been put into the layout of the grounds. There were various plateaux around a central apex, in the middle of which was a pond containing an array of colourful fish. Water trickled in various directions, finding its way into smaller pools scattered around on lower levels. Little clusters of miniature trees and neatly clipped hedges were arranged around small, secluded enclaves offering a tranquillity enhanced by the gentle sound of running water. Having taken a thorough look around the whole area and noted to her satisfaction that she had the grounds entirely to herself, Sophie chose an inlet that faced the south and took a seat therein. As she did so, she became aware of music beginning to play. She could hear the sound of the harp and the flute, but as inside the clinic could not tell exactly where it was coming from.

There was no denying that this was a beautiful place, and she could not help feeling really content there. It was such a contrast to her last experience of a visit to a health establishment. She had not needed to visit a hospital, a clinic or even a doctor's surgery since the awful day in July 2005 when she had received the news that her mother had been taken to hospital after suffering a suspected heart attack while shopping in Hayward's Heath. Lucky was out, playing golf at the time and she had called a taxi to take her straight to the hospital. She remembered urging the driver to get them there as soon as possible, but it was a wet day, there were road works, and heavy traffic. Over an hour elapsed between receiving the call and arriving at the hospital. She recalled the anxious wait in the casualty reception, and the confusion as some road accident victims were being brought in at the same time. She remembered the serious look on the face of the nurse who had led her away into a small, bare room, and her opening remark: 'I'm afraid I have some bad news for you…' After that everything was a blur. The hospital staff had called a taxi to take her home. Her father had still not returned when she got back. He had stopped for a drink in the golf course clubhouse, and when he did appear he was very drunk and did not take the news in properly until the following day. It was the eve of her mother's birthday, and a big surprise party had been arranged in *Paradise*. In the midst of her shock and grief

Sophie had had to call the guests and break the news to them. She hadn't managed to get through to everybody and two couples had turned up the following evening.

Sophie, who was nineteen at the time, had been inconsolable for months, and had not returned to Sussex university for the second year of her music degree in the autumn. Her mother's death came less than a year after that of her grandfather, whose legacy had enabled them to buy the mansion which Lucky had renamed *Paradise*. Her father's reaction to his wife's death had puzzled Sophie. He had certainly not made his grief very apparent, although he had been strangely quiet and subdued for a while. For sure, he was a man who had been hardened by his experiences of life, which at one time had included involvements with some rather incompetent criminals. Sophie knew little about what had occurred; nor did she wish to know. After all, this was something that was firmly in the past. And her father was now her only living relative.

Sophie's train of thought was interrupted by a single chime from a distant spire. She went back inside the clinic to see whether her father was ready to leave. There was no sign of Lucky in the waiting room, so Sophie returned to the room that had been assigned to her. She pressed the buzzer again. This time the call was answered by an older man wearing a smart suit. She enquired as to her father's whereabouts.

'He'll be with you shortly, Miss Hanson,' came the reply. The man held out his hand. 'My name's Dr Braithwaite.' He was a short, plump man, with white hair, an equally white beard, and a benevolent face. Given a red outfit he would have made a convincing Father Christmas. He smiled reassuringly.

'Pleased to meet you,' Sophie replied, a little perplexed.

'Do, please sit down,' the doctor began, indicating the chaise longue. Sophie obliged, and the doctor pulled up a nearby chair.

'Your father has asked me to have a word with you,' continued the doctor. 'I understand you have some reservations about enrolling for treatment here. I'm sure I can put your mind at rest.'

'Dr Braithwaite, I don't know what my father has told you, but I have no intention of coming here for treatment.'

The doctor looked benignly at her.

'You're very young. You have time on your side at the moment. All the same…' He paused for a moment. 'It's nothing to do with me, I know, but your father is willing to spend over a million pounds to enable you to come here. Surely you owe it to him to take just a few minutes listening to what I have to say.'

Sophie felt unable to protest. The doctor, understanding her silence as acquiescence, continued:

'Miss Hanson, believe me, here at the Walton Foundation we are very proud of what we've achieved. It has taken years of research by gifted and dedicated scientists in a number of countries. But in fact the breakthrough was made here in Britain, right here in this clinic.'

He could see that she was unmoved.

'Let me tell you a little more about the treatment. Firstly, you are given a very thorough medical examination, to make sure you are completely healthy. Provided the results are satisfactory, you are given an injection of the substance PLH, which in this country is only available here and at our sister clinic in Staffordshire. The substance is comprised of mainly natural ingredients. If you decide to enrol here, I can go into more detail with you. However, under the terms of the Health Enhancing Substances Act I am not permitted to divulge exactly how PLH is produced. Suffice it to say that in any case the explanation would be quite meaningless to a non-scientist. I assure you that we have every reason to believe that PLH is completely risk-free, and the process by which it is introduced to the body is totally painless. The initial effect is similar to that of a general anaesthetic, and you will feel a little groggy afterwards. That's why we recommend that patients are accompanied by a relative or friend who can see them safely home after their first visit.'

The doctor paused. Sophie had said nothing.

'Do you have any questions so far?' he enquired.

'No,' she replied.

'Good. Moving on to the question of the benefits of the treatment, these, I assure you, are truly amazing. Allow me to demonstrate.'

He produced a sheet of glossy paper on which two photos of the same man had been set side by side. The man had thick, dark hair, and looked to be in his mid-fifties.

Dr Braithwaite smiled knowingly.

'These are photographs of Dr Giles Walsingham, of whom you may have heard. He's the owner of the clinic, and was instrumental in developing PLH. I would introduce you to him, but he's not here today. I believe he's gone fishing,' he thought aloud. 'Tell me, what would you say is the difference between these two photographs?'

Sophie studied them for a few moments. Despite her reservations, she could not help warming to Dr Braithwaite. There was something about his demeanour that was very engaging. Perhaps it was the cheekiness of his grin, or the twinkle in his eyes as he spoke. He was a man to whom few people took exception.

'Only the haircut,' she concluded.

'Yes, indeed!' he chortled. 'Anything else?'

She shook her head. The doctor leaned forward so that he could point to the photos.

'This one,' he began, indicating the photo on the right, 'was taken in the year 2004.' He slid his finger to the left. 'Whereas that one,' he said, turning to look her directly in the eyes 'was taken last month.'

Sophie did not admit to being impressed, but her expression suggested she was, at least a little.

'You see, there's no doubt the treatment works,' the doctor resumed. The very first injection of PLH immediately arrests the ageing process, enabling the recipients to live for hundreds, potentially thousands of years. Furthermore, PLH prevents the onset of all non-contagious disease, as well as the vast majority of contagious diseases. Not only do you stay alive, you also stay healthy. All you have to do is to return to the clinic every six months for what one might think of as a "top-up".'

He paused, silently compelling Sophie to respond. At last she spoke:

'But you do die eventually?'

Dr Braithwaite nodded solemnly.

'Yes, there's no way, of course, that PLH or anything else can prevent accidents or death by violence. And if after so many years you do fccl that thc timc has come to grow old, then all you would need to do would be to stop receiving the injections, and the effects would wear off.'

'Can you be sure of that?'

'We are completely confident that would be the case, although we can't prove it yet, because no one has decided to discontinue their treatment.' He smiled proudly. 'Not one, out of almost a thousand patients.'

'But this could lead to an enormous problem with over-population, once it becomes too widespread.'

'That's a very valid point,' the doctor agreed, 'and one which has not been lost on the government. That's why the treatment is so expensive. It's regrettable that such a tremendous blessing has to be restricted, but it simply would not be practicable to enable everyone who wanted to live indefinitely to do so. I'm afraid the only sensible solution is to limit it to those who are in the privileged position of being able to afford it.'

'But just think of all the good that could have been done in the world if the money had been used to address the real problems, rather than encouraging those who are already fortunate to be greedy.'

Dr Braithwaite sat back and looked kindly at Sophie.

'Ah, Miss Hanson, I see that you are a person who thinks a great deal and cares about the state of the world. Well, as it happens, a large proportion of the clinic's fees are, by law, redirected to charities which deal with alleviating the problems caused by poverty.' He pondered for a moment. 'I'll leave you with this thought. Consider how much good someone with your outlook could do given the opportunity to live indefinitely. Miss Hanson, I understand why your father should feel as he does. If you were my daughter, I would beg you to reconsider. I do hope that you will at least give some thought to what I've said. And now, I think we have kept your father waiting long enough.'

Chapter 3

The barmaid placed the two plates on the wooden table. Sophie thanked her and began her meal. She wriggled slightly along the seat, trying to escape the unwanted protection afforded by the parasol that shrouded most of their corner of the pub garden. She glanced across at her father, who had not responded in any way to the arrival of the food. She could just about see the top of his head over the newspaper he was pretending to read. Lucky had various ways of communicating his vexation. Choosing to sit in the shade in the knowledge that his daughter preferred the sunshine was one tactic. Using the newspaper as a barrier to communication was another. Behaving in a discourteous manner towards other people also seemed to serve this purpose. And yet, Sophie reflected, she was the one who had reason to be annoyed. Her father was putting pressure on her to act against her beliefs, and had set up the approach by Dr Braithwaite without her consent. And now he was behaving as though he had cause to be upset with her.

Moreover, Sophie was disgruntled that she had found Dr Braithwaite's arguments quite persuasive, to the extent that she had agreed to continue to review her reservations. She had not realized that the clinic kept only part of its revenue. Certainly, if she allowed her father to pay for the treatment, a considerable sum of money that would otherwise remain part of his fortune indefinitely would be released for worthwhile causes. And yes, the doctor's final comment had hit home. Who could say what she might be able to achieve given hundreds of years in which to work? She was prepared to accept that her objections in principle might be misguided. But there was more to it than that. Something was making her very uncomfortable about the whole idea. It was an inexplicable perception, an apprehension that it was not possible to justify rationally, an intuition one might say. She just *felt* that something was going to go badly wrong as a result of her father's decision, and that if she took the same course of action the situation would somehow be compounded.

Sophie realized that she had nearly finished her meal, whereas her father was yet to start his.

'Dad, your food's getting cold.'

Lucky waited a few seconds, then replied:

'I know.'

Then he turned over a page of the newspaper to signify that he would discontinue his supposed preoccupation with it in his own time and not as a result of his daughter's prompting.

Sophie had still not mentioned the detour for which she had been hoping to obtain her father's consent. She felt sure that to do so now would create a further opportunity for him to withhold co-operation in support of his stance. Maybe they should get the argument out in the open. She was considering how to bring up the subject, when her father put down the paper and began his meal. They ate in silence for a few minutes. Just as Sophie was putting her knife and fork down on her plate, Lucky looked across at her and began:

'That doctor, what was his name?'

'Dr. Braithwaite.'

'Yes. A very clever man, don't you think?'

'Sure.'

'And interesting to talk to?'

'Very,' Sophie acknowledged. Then, spurred on by the additional irritation inspired by her father's renewed probing, she added:

'But you shouldn't have got him to speak to me, not without asking me. That wasn't fair, Dad'.

Lucky's face became flusher; his expression turned to a glare.

'Oh really?' he fumed. 'Do you know how many people would love to be given the opportunity you've got? I wish the treatment had been available when I was your age. Do you know what your trouble is? You only think about yourself and your bloody ideals. What about me? You're all I have. You're the only person I care for. And you expect me to sit and watch you grow old. And then I'll be alone for years and years. Is that what you think is fair, eh?'

He thrust his cutlery down on top of his meal and pushed the plate forward, as evidence of the loss of appetite that had been brought on by his daughter's admonition.

Sophie sat for a few moments, a pained expression on her face. Then she responded, calmly:

'I'm sorry, Dad, but I can't do something I don't believe in just out of consideration for you.'

There was no reply. Sophie noticed how dry her throat felt.

'I'm going to have another drink. Would you like one?' she asked.

Lucky shook his head.

The pub was crowded inside, and Sophie had to wait at the bar for several minutes for her orange juice and lemonade. On a shelf behind her, above the noise of the chatter, she could hear the coverage of the test match, until this was interrupted by a news flash about the latest crisis in the Middle East. Returning to the garden, she was surprised to see a man sitting opposite her father. She did not recognise him at first, but as she got closer she caught a glimpse of the side of his face and was able to identify him. She stopped in her tracks, and mouthed his name:

'Jock Pope.'

Sophie remembered her previous experience of Jock Pope. Again it was a chance encounter in a pub. She and her father had begun a meal on their own early one evening, and had been spotted by Jock who had just finished eating with some companions. Lucky and Jock had talked all evening, reminiscing about their adolescent days and the pranks they had played on people, some of which struck Sophie as being rather distasteful. Feeling bored and excluded from the conversation, she had circumvented the pub in the vain hope of finding someone she knew. Pausing by the jukebox before returning, she strained to overhear Lucky and Jock's conversation, without making them aware of her presence. She could not hear her father at all, but some of Jock's words were audible, albeit slurred now, as the rapidly consumed Newcastle Browns took effect. She heard enough to confirm her suspicions. There was no doubting the significance of the terms 'GBH' and 'in the nick'.

Sophie had no wish to spend any more time in the company of Jock Pope. And her father would probably stay there for hours, eventually declaring that it was time to go home, and would surely decree that it was too late now to do anything else.

An idea came to her. She turned round and went back inside the pub and asked the whereabouts of the public telephone. The barman pointed to the far side of the room. Through a cloud of cigar smoke she could see that the phone was in use. A cry of 'howzat' from the direction of the television informed her that the cricket coverage had resumed. Sophie felt a little shiver. Was it perhaps that the temperature inside the pub was that much cooler than the furnace outside, she wondered?

Suddenly the phone was free. A card pinned to the wall above provided the number of the local taxi firm.

A minute later Sophie was striding boldly towards the corner of the garden, where Lucky and Jock were still deep in conversation. She could see that her father was much more cheerful now. He even chuckled at something Jock said just as she arrived.

'You took your time,' Lucky commented.

'Yes, I made a phone call.'

'Oh?'

'I've decided to go and visit Mum's grave. I've called a taxi to take me there. I'll see you at home later on.'

The anticipated disapproval did not materialise.

'Okay,' said Lucky, 'see you later.'

Presumably the prospect of spending some time with Jock had changed her father's outlook, Sophie reflected. Perhaps he was pleased she was leaving them alone together; it would enable them to talk more freely. She did not want to imagine what they might discuss. Reluctant to acknowledge Jock in any way, she decided to wait inside the pub.

'Before you go, Sophie, get us a couple of pints of lager,' Lucky called after her. 'Here,' he said, thrusting a ten pound coin into her hand.

Inside, the volume of the customers' babble had increased. There was some excitement in the air. Sussex batsman Tony Watson had just completed his maiden century for England prior to the tea interval, the barman informed her. Someone somewhere was operating a remote control, because as Sophie stood waiting for the drinks she had ordered the television near the bar was spouting gibberish...'second number six, Stealth Bomber, the even money favourite'.... 'Henry's cat's hobbies were eating, sleeping, eating, sleeping and sleeping'... finally it settled down to the sound of the familiar voice of local newsreader Pauline Willis. She was saying something about a man who had been found shot dead by a pond.

'That'll be seven pounds twenty please, miss,' said the barman. Sophie smiled at the young man and presented him with the ten pound coin.

A word from the direction of the screen behind her attracted her attention. Gerontology. She turned to face the screen. It was a word that she had heard very recently, and she had puzzled over its meaning. The man who had been murdered had been responsible for significant developments in the field of gerontology.

'Your change, miss.'

'Thank you.' Turning to the barman, Sophie accepted the change and picked up the two pints of lager. The pint in her left hand had been poured carelessly and had spilled over, leaving the rim of the glass rather slippery.

Sophie's mind was still on the riddle of the expert in gerontology. She turned, looked back at the screen and saw...a face...a face she recognised...a face she knew now, but a few hours earlier had never seen before…a single face which she had previously seen in duplicate…the face of Dr Giles Walsingham.

A moment later a crash could be heard which momentarily silenced the hubbub of the customers' banter. It was the sound of breaking glass – the sound of the pint glass which Sophie had been holding in her left hand smashing as it hit the cold, stone floor of the bar.

Chapter 4

'Excuse me, could we stop at the village shop in Manning's Heath?' Sophie asked the driver. 'I just want to buy some flowers.'

'Right you are, miss,' came the reply.

They passed the South Lodge Hotel on their left. Sophie glanced through the gateway as she always did when she came along the Brighton Road. She did not see anything noteworthy, just the driveway and the bushes which bordered it. Nor did she expect to see anything unusual. Her action was simply an acknowledgement of the fact that this was the place where she had first met William.

Sophie returned to her thoughts. Everything had happened at once in the pub. The revelation of the victim's identity, and her dropping of the glass had coincided with the arrival of the taxi driver. The kindly barman had ushered her on her way, assuring her that he would replace the second drink and take it out to the garden. Sophie wondered what her father's reaction would be when he heard the news of Dr Walsingham's murder. He would be sure to curse the protest groups who had opposed the clinic's activities, even if they denied any responsibility for the scientist's death. It was unlikely that he could be persuaded to take any precautions in case the extremists turned their attentions to the patients. Her father was too used to riding his luck and getting away with it. He was inclined to confuse caution with cowardice, as her grandfather had once observed.

The taxi pulled into the forecourt of the village shop.

'I won't be a moment,' Sophie assured the driver.

The choice of flowers was an easy one, given that there was a solitary bunch of irises left on display, and she was back at the car within a minute. Acting on an impulse, she enquired:

'Have you time to take me round to Handcross, so we can come all the way along Hammerpond Road?'

The driver looked at her curiously. 'It's the long way round, young lady. It would be cheaper to go straight on up the road.'

'That's okay,' replied Sophie. 'It's just that it will bring back memories,' she explained.

The driver assented without further ado, and Sophie soon found herself starting to reminisce. She and her mother had made many journeys along Hammerpond Road, sometimes on foot, sometimes on horseback. The road undulated constantly, and it had taken a while before they had become familiar with what lay beyond each crest. On either side were stylish country dwellings, unique in design, which always seemed strangely devoid of occupants. At one point the local golf course came very close to the side of the road. The only evidence of this was a small green which nestled in a hollow some way below the level of the road. Sometimes a golf ball would plop mysteriously down, occasionally plugging in the ground because of the bogginess of the surface. Sophie and her mother had scrutinised the trees without ever spotting the tee from which the golfers delivered their shots. Then there was the pond itself, which came right up against the roadside just at the point where Hammerpond Road was at its narrowest. Somehow the murkiness of the water enhanced the attractiveness of the pond and helped to generate its unfathomable appeal.

The taxi's journey through this haven of memories culminated at St. John's church in Coolham. Sophie asked the time; it was half past five. She glanced into the cemetery and noted with some disappointment that an old man was tending one of the graves. She really needed complete solitude.

'That'll be twenty-two pounds, please,' said the driver. Sophie handed over twenty-five pounds and waived the change.

'Can you come back for me around half past eight?' she asked.

'Certainly miss,' came the reply. The driver made no comment, but his surprised expression suggested he was wondering why she needed such a long time.

Sophie walked through the graveyard, and on round to the back of the church where the more recent burials had taken place. Approaching the grave, she knelt down, and carefully placed the irises by the headstone.

'Hello mum,' she whispered. 'I'll be with you very shortly.'

Then she stood up, and began to wander round the cemetery, taking in the names of those who had been laid to rest there, subtracting one date from another to work out their age at death, looking to see who had loved them. All the while she was checking the progress of the old man nearby, and observing the road for any other visitors. At last she was granted the freedom she needed.

Sophie settled down by the headstone, kneeling with her head bowed as though at prayer. She began, as always, by re-reading the inscription:

IRIS MARY HANSON (24 July 1948 – 23 July 2005) much loved wife of Andrew and mother of Sophie. *Life will never be the same without you.*

Sophie nodded, in acknowledgement of the enduring truth of the epitaph. She arranged the irises meticulously in the little pot which sat beside the headstone in readiness. Then she opened her bag and took out a small mirror with a sky blue frame and handle, which had been a present from her mother when she was thirteen. Raising it to within inches of her face, she started to look intently into it, contemplating her own features in what would have seemed to any onlooker like a bizarre act of vain folly. She focused on the centre of her face, the distinctive Roman nose, and above all the deep, blue eyeballs with oversized pupils, concentrating on the features she had shared with her mother, Iris… Sophie recalled the explanation her grandfather had given her once for the choice of name: 'What else could we have called her once we saw those eyes?' The recollection brought a smile to Sophie's face, a smile which she began to manipulate, allowing her mouth to open slightly, turning her lips fractionally inwards or outwards, loosening or tightening the muscles in her cheeks. At the same time she experimented with the position of her head, inclining it slightly to one side as though listening carefully to someone, or tilting it forward so that the eyeballs rolled to the top of their sockets to maintain the constancy of her gaze. All the while she was searching for an image with which she was satisfied and that she would be able to retain.

Minutes passed by and many more followed, but Sophie was oblivious to the passage of time or the fact that the sun to her right was beginning to tickle the tops of the trees, or even to the discomfort inflicted on her body by the rigidity of her stance. Finally she dared to close her eyes for the briefest of moments…then again a few seconds later…and again…and many more times until eventually she could keep them closed without fear of losing the vividness of the picture her mind's eye had gone to such lengths to create.

And then she began to murmur, softly, gently, in a voice which exuded warmth, uttering a few words at a time: ordinary phrases, often repeated by ordinary people, which had however been rendered unique by virtue of their intonation…'it's only me'…'what's the matter?'… 'stay safe'…each became a sound more beautiful than any music. Finally she sang her own name, and listened for the echo within her head. She called again, and this time the cry was taken up by the picture to which her mind had been clinging, thus uniting sound and vision: 'Sophie….Sophie…oh, Sophie, how lovely to see you! But you look upset, my child. What's the matter? Come here, let me give you a hug!'

The relief was overwhelming.

'Oh, Mum, it's been so long!'

'Have things been difficult? Yes, they have, haven't they? Oh dear! I wish I could help. What is it now? Come on now, tell me.'

'Oh it's just…well you know what Dad's like. I mean he's found his paradise and he wants to stay there forever, or at least as long as he possibly can, and I just don't think it's right. And anyway, I want us all to be together again sooner or later.'

'And so we will be, my dear, so we will be. Listen, how's the music going? Have you got lots of pupils?'

'I've got twelve now, and another two starting next term.'

'Oh, that's great! You know, I do miss hearing you play the piano. Are you practising every day?'

'Almost.'

'Good. And how's William?'

'Oh, he's…well, the same.'

'Has he asked you to marry him yet?'

'No. I don't think William's ready for marriage just yet.'

'But he does love you?'

'Yes, I believe he does.'

'Is he working yet?'

'No, but he's going to start at a practice up in the city in the autumn. His parents are really pleased. They've paid for him to go on a space holiday next month.'

'Holidays in space! Well, I never! Still, they said it would happen, didn't they?'

'Yes, it's quite common in America now, and it's quite safe. They've had no problems at all.'

'That's good. William is such a charming young man! And such an adventurer! I do hope he stays safe, for your sake as well, of course. I always thought you made such a lovely couple. You make sure he deserves you, though!'

'Do you think he does deserve me?'

'I think so.'

'Oh Mum, it's so good to hear your voice. It was difficult this time…getting through to you, I mean.'

'I know. Listen, I have an idea. Next time bring some of my perfume with you. That'll make it easier.'

'Of course! Why didn't I think of that before?'

'And now, my child, you must go. Stay safe, and remember I love you.'

'I love you too.'

Sophie felt the warmth of her mother's arms around her. At the same time, she felt a tap on the shoulder. A little startled, she opened her eyes and looked round.

'Sorry, miss. I tried calling you, but I couldn't get your attention. I've been waiting some time. It's gone half past eight.'

Chapter 5

Through a window in the music room Sophie looked across the forecourt towards the row of seven garages, none of which had seen action since the day before. A small bird was hopping around near the fountain in the centre of the forecourt, otherwise all was still in *Paradise*. Another day of uninterrupted sunshine had been promised, and already the heat was almost visible.

Returning to the piano, Sophie resumed her attempts to remove the label 'unplayable' which she had attached to Scriabin's *Vers la flamme*. The dark, brooding tones with which the piece began were soon cut short by two higher-pitched notes in quick succession from an altogether different source, signifying something far less profound; the security system at the front gates had recognised the vehicle William was driving and had allowed him to enter *Paradise*.

William's ascent of the steps to the entrance to the mansion coincided with Sophie's arrival at the front door. The difference between the level of the last step and the floor of the hallway compensated for William's extra couple of inches in height, thereby facilitating the quick kiss they exchanged before any words were spoken.

'Surprise!' exclaimed William.

'I thought you were going kite surfing today.'

'So did I, but Trevor can't make it after all, and I didn't want to go on my own, so here I am. I'm all yours for the day. What would you like to do?'

'Oh. I don't know. I ought to finish my practice first. Perhaps we could have a swim before lunch. Let's use the outdoor pool, as it's such a lovely day. And then we could go out this afternoon. Take me for a romantic walk in the countryside.'

'You're on.' He smiled. 'Can I come and listen to your practising?'

'Only if you promise to sit still! Last time you kept rustling your newspaper, and I couldn't concentrate.'

'Hmm! Perhaps I had better sit and have a coffee while you finish. What are you playing, anyway?'

'*Vers la flamme*, by Scriabin.'

'Oh yes, one of my very favourite tunes,' he joked. William looked closely at Sophie, feasting his eyes on the flowing locks of golden hair adorning her shoulders which had turned many a head.

'I like your hair down,' he concluded.

'I thought you preferred it when I wear it in a bun.'

'Well yes, when you're dressing up for an evening out, I do. But just now, in your natural habitat, as it were, you look great just as you are.'

'In my natural habitat, eh?' she replied. 'You make me sound like some sort of wild animal.' She laughed, and playfully clawed at him with paw-like hands. He joined in the game, seizing her wrists and forcing her arms wide of her body; then he pushed her back against the wall of the hallway and began growling loudly in her ear.

'William, don't! William, my dad might come down the stairs at any moment.'

'Grrh! So? Arrgh!'

'Look, let's go outside. You can make as much noise as you like there. Come on, please, I don't want to wake my dad up.'

'Please, oh William, please,' he mimicked.

She managed to duck from under his grasp, and in an instant was round the corner of the hallway, scurrying down the corridor, passing the dining room on her left, the lounge and TV room on her right and finally the kitchen on her left, with William right behind her all the way, deliberately allowing her to keep fractionally ahead. Reaching the back door, she flung it open and raced down the steps, across the croquet lawn and through the row of trees which led to an untended part of the grounds. Only here did William inject the extra pace required to catch his quarry, lifting her upwards as he did so, going to ground himself first before bringing her down on top of him to ensure that he didn't hurt her. Here the grass was tall enough, and the surrounding bushes ample enough, that even if there had been anyone on the estate they would not have been able to observe what followed.

'Come on, we had better get back,' said Sophie, sitting up in the grass. 'Dad will probably be up by now.'

She stood up and began brushing herself down. William picked at her back. Then they turned their attention to the little scraps of foliage which had attached themselves to his clothing.

'We've been for a walk, okay,' said Sophie, preparing William for her father's possible enquiries.

'Naturally,' William replied, grinning. 'I'm sure your father would be deeply shocked if he knew what we had been up to in the grass. I'm quite sure he would never have dreamt of doing such things when he was young.'

Sophie pulled a face.

'What's the matter?'

'I wouldn't like to say how many girlfriends my dad had before he married my mum. I don't suppose he kept count. Anyway, as far as he's concerned there's one rule for him and another for me. I'm still trying to put him straight about that. Still, what happens between you and me is strictly private, okay?'

William's response took the form of a solemn salute.

'Your wish is my command,' he added.

As they approached the house hand in hand, William observed:

'Your father is up.'

'How do you know?'

'Because the back door is shut.'

'You mean you didn't close it behind you.'

'Nor did you!'

Back inside the mansion, the sound from the television room indicated Lucky's whereabouts. The couple appeared in the doorway.

'Morning, Mr Hanson.'

Lucky nodded in acknowledgement and wagged a finger at the television.

'Cricket's about to start,' he pointed out.

'Oh excellent!' exclaimed William. 'Sophie, you don't mind if I keep your dad company for a while, do you?' he asked, taking a seat.

'I suppose not. I'll go and finish my practice.' She turned to go. 'Don't forget we were going to have a swim before lunch, though,' she added softly.

Passing through the hallway Sophie noticed that *The Independent* was protruding from the letterbox; she was reminded of what had been troubling her. Pulling the newspaper free, she began to scan the front page, expecting to see a reference to the murder of Dr Walsingham inside. However she was surprised to find that the article started on the front page itself. *'Pioneer scientist found murdered'* read the headline. Some of the details were already familiar to her from the previous day's news bulletin. The doctor's body had been found by a fellow angler at a fishery near his home in Ardingly. His assailant had clearly taken him by surprise; he had been shot three times and had died instantly. The police had sealed off the whole area to look for forensic evidence. The suspicion that there was a link with the protest groups campaigning against the Walton Foundation was being investigated, although spokespersons from the groups had vehemently denied any involvement in the murder. The article went on to give details of Dr Walsingham's glittering career and his groundbreaking contribution to research into the ageing process, and how he and the late Dr Philip Tonbridge had set up the Walton Foundation in 2004. Details were given of some of the wealthiest people in the world who were known to have received treatment there. A profile of the scientist, a chronology of his achievements, and some tributes from other members of his profession could be found on page seven. Sophie looked only briefly at the inside page, however. The article had not told her what she had hoped, namely that the murder was unconnected with opponents of the Walton Foundation. Sophie imagined what it must be like to be sitting beside a pond without a care in the world one moment, only to be confronted by someone with a gun and realise your time had come the next. She shuddered, and only then did she recall the curious shiver which she had felt inside the pub the previous day.

Sophie still did not know whether her father was aware of the scientist's demise. Lucky had remained with Jock until closing time and she had gone to bed prior to his return. For a moment she considered whether to take the newspaper in to him. However she knew that if he had not heard the news his reaction would be one of anger, and she did not want to spoil his enjoyment of the cricket coverage, especially since William was watching it with him. Cricket was one of the few things they had in common, and Sophie was keen to encourage a better understanding between them. In any case she wanted to take her mind off the matter. So she chose instead to return to her musical endeavours.

The technical demands of Scriabin's composition compelled her to concentrate on her playing, but this activity did not have the effect of a distraction. Indeed the sombre, anxious mood of the piece served only to exaggerate her own inexplicable apprehension. A single bleep from the intercom arrested her progress with the force of an electric shock.

William's voice followed:

'Sophie, quick, come and see this.'

A glance at her watch confirmed that they would be watching the lunchtime news.

'So you knew?' enquired Lucky. 'Why the hell didn't you tell me?'

'I've hardly seen you, have I?' she retorted. 'Did you know him?'

'I met him when I went there for the medical.' He paused. 'Those bloody protestors are behind this, I bet you any money you like.' He slammed an empty mug which he had been holding down on the table. 'Bastards!' he declared.

'What will happen to the Walton Foundation now?' Sophie asked.

Lucky was still fuming silently. William took it upon himself to answer:

'Apparently the doctor was due to retire shortly, and was going to hand over to some of the other consultants.'

'How do you know that?' Lucky wanted to know.

'Because I read about it this morning.'

'So you knew as well?'

'Yes, I didn't realise you didn't.'

Lucky's face was becoming pinker, his exasperation at not having been given the news aggravating his wrath. William tried to appease him:

'Listen, old boy, it wasn't a conspiracy, you know. It's just that nobody happened to mention it.'

Lucky shook his head and left the room.

'Was it something I said?' William asked Sophie.

'I don't suppose he took it too well when you called him "old boy". Why don't you call him "Lucky" like everyone else?'

William's response served to remind her that he had answered this question once before. Looking up eagerly at Sophie, he allowed his tongue to hang out, and began to pant rapidly and noisily. Then he emitted a plaintive, high-pitched yelping sound.

Sophie giggled. 'I remember,' she acknowledged. 'The black poodle you had as a child.'

He nodded.

'Very good, I'm impressed, even if your memory did need jogging.'

Sophie put one hand on each of William's shoulders and looked fondly down at him. He grinned up at her in a way which suggested he was still in doggy mode.

'William,' she began earnestly, 'are you ever going to take life seriously?'

'I sincerely hope not!' he replied, with an unwavering smile. 'Come on, let's go for a swim.'

Chapter 6

A small, grey head with dark eyes and pricked ears popped up over the top of the fence, pausing momentarily. The rest of the body and a bushy tail followed and a second later a flash of grey and white was skipping across the lawn in the direction of the trees. The squirrel barely noticed a larger dog-like figure squatting nearby in the early evening sun, its outstretched paws bisected by a pointed nozzle containing sharp, unclean teeth.

A door opened and the fox stood up abruptly, stared directly for several seconds at the two people descending the steps, then turned and trotted off towards the cover of the bushes.

'So who else is going to be there this evening?' William asked Sophie.

'Anita's parents and some friends of theirs. By the way, Anita's thinking of doing a law course, and she wants your advice.'

'Well as long as she doesn't expect me to remember anything just at the moment. It's about two months since my finals. It will all have been forgotten now.'

Sophie looked a little alarmed.

'But what will happen when you start your job?'

'Oh, that's not for weeks yet. I've got my space trip to think about before that. I suppose I had better look through a few books the day before I start, though.'

Sophie still looked concerned as she took her seat in the yellow MG which William had borrowed from his father for the evening.

'Don't worry. It will come flooding back when it's needed,' he assured her.

As William settled in the driver's seat he paused to take a proper look at Sophie. His eyes greeted what they held with complete approval: the deftly applied eye shadow, the tasteful scarf, the sparkling sapphire resting on her nape, all evoked a look of satisfaction bordering on jubilation.

William knew that Sophie liked to hear him speak French. He was able to affect an authentic accent in a deep, sexy voice:

'Oh, ma Sophie, que tu es belle ce soir!'

She acknowledged the compliment with a smile. Then she leaned across and whispered in his ear:

'Je t'adore, mon amour.'

Their journey took them through the villages near *Paradise* which Sophie knew so well. They passed through Nuthurst and paused outside the Black Horse pub. It was here that they had first kissed, and it had become a tradition to recreate the moment.

'Christmas eve, 2004,' Sophie reminded William solemnly.

'You're so sentimental!' he observed.

Then he took her hands in his, kissed each in turn, and drew her to him. They exchanged a single gentle kiss, as natural as their first.

'You know, you definitely kissed my right hand first.'

'No, no, I assure you it was your left hand first!'

'We'll never know for sure!'

William turned the key in the ignition and put the vehicle in gear. As they started to move off, Sophie suddenly remarked:

'I've just realised something. The Walton Foundation was named after Dr *Wal*singham and Dr *Ton*bridge.'

William looked bemused.

'Whatever made you think of that?'

'It's been on my mind a lot today.'

'Have they made any progress with the investigation?'

'No, they're none the wiser. It's been over a week now. I read in the local paper that the protest group has condemned the murder, and is adamant that there is no connection with any of their members. They even appealed for whoever did it to give themselves up.'

'What about the death threats?'

'They don't help much, as they were typed and sent anonymously. The police are advising all those employed at the Walton Foundation to take extra security precautions, though.'

'Whatever could motivate someone to commit murder over an issue like that?'

'My dad reckons it's down to jealousy.'

'That sounds a bit unlikely.'

'Yes, that was my reaction. But I've been thinking about it. Imagine if someone were an extremely jealous person, and they desperately wanted to live indefinitely, but say for instance there was no way they could afford it. They would be sure to resent the fact that someone else could have what they wanted. It would drive them mad. It might even become an obsession.'

'But would it really affect someone enough to bring them to commit murder?'

'Possibly.'

Sophie paused, then asked:

'William, do you believe in destiny?'

He chuckled.

'I don't know. I don't think so. Do you?'

She nodded.

'Remember I told you about how I felt sure when I first met you at the South Lodge Hotel that you were going to play a big part in my life, even though I hardly had the chance to speak to you. And then a year later you turned up at Sussex university.'

'Yes, that is strange, but it could be just coincidence.'

'I suppose so, but that's not the only time I've had such convictions. And recently I've had this growing feeling that something awful is going to happen as a result of Dad's involvement with the Walton Foundation, and now on the very day he starts his treatment the owner of the clinic is murdered.'

William considered this revelation. Although he appreciated the oddness of this occurrence, he felt sure there must be a rational explanation.

'I think your imagination's doing overtime,' he concluded eventually.

Sophie did not reply. William took such opportunities as the winding country road permitted to glance across at her.

The levity which had been evident a few minutes earlier had gone. On the contrary, she seemed withdrawn. Reaching a straight stretch of road, William took her right hand in his left, and was surprised by how cold it felt. He pulled in to the side of the road.

'Are you all right?'

For a moment Sophie sat completely motionless, then she turned to William and said:

'Yes, I'm okay.' However her answer lacked conviction. 'I just feel nervous about this evening,' she added.

'Why? These people are your friends.'

'I don't know why.'

William looked at her, somewhat bemused.

'Sophie, you're a funny one sometimes.'

'You think so?'

'I know so. Come on, let's go.'

He checked over his right shoulder, before setting the sports car in motion.

'William, do we have to go this evening?' Sophie asked in a tentative voice.

'Of course. We can't let them down now. It's okay, we're nearly there.'

'William, look after me this evening.' There was a hint of urgency about her request.

'Of course.'

He glanced across at her. This time his expression spoke less of bewilderment and more of concern.

Chapter 7

William was seated at six o'clock around the large circular dining table with Sophie at five o'clock and Anita at seven. The young man was relishing being surrounded by such beauty. It was remarkable how similar the two friends were. They had more than once been mistaken for sisters. Anita was listening intently to William's attempt to convey his passion for kite surfing when a gentle whirring sound caught their attention. He watched with evident surprise as the centre of the table began its steady descent to the kitchen below. Four segments contained within the exterior section of the table converged to form a temporary replacement.

'That's what happens when you have a dad who's an inventor,' Anita explained. 'Things often happen that you weren't expecting. It's great fun,' she enthused, smiling. She looked across at her father, seated at twelve o'clock. 'Even if he is a little ostentatious.'

'Well, I'm not as bad as some people I know in that respect,' Mr Burkin replied. 'I haven't got a different car for each day of the week.'

'Henry, stop it, you're embarrassing Sophie,' his wife Melissa intervened from one o'clock.

'Ah, Sophie knows I'm only joking, don't you my dear?'

Sophie smiled weakly.

'It's okay, people are always pulling my leg because of my dad's eccentricities.'

She glanced at William, expecting him to add some amusing witticism. However William's attention was elsewhere. He was leaning back in his chair, trying not to make it too obvious he was looking under the table.

Anita had noticed William's puzzlement, and undertook to explain.

'Oh, part of the floor goes down too, ahead of the centre of the table, and then the hole is covered in the same way as the one in the middle of the table. '

William signified his understanding with a nod. At that moment the whirring sound began again and the central segments began to retract. The aroma wafted upwards through the gap in the middle of the table and reached the diners ahead of the food itself.

'Japanese,' announced Anita. 'We've hired this crew before, and they are really something. What are their names again, mummy?'

'Isao and Hisaho,' came the reply.

Anita giggled.

'I'm laughing at Mummy's pronunciation,' she explained. 'I've been learning Japanese. I want to go there next summer.'

'How exciting!' exclaimed William.

'Not as exciting as holidaying in space!' Anita replied, with a look of unrestrained envy. 'How does it feel to be a budding astronaut?'

'Great. I can't wait.'

Leaning slightly towards him, she whispered:

'Got any room for a stowaway?'

They laughed in unison.

'I know someone who went on a space trip a year or so ago,' said Grant, an American friend of the family who was seated on the other side of Anita. 'She kept a journal and had it published when she got back to earth. She did very well out of it. You should do that too, William.'

William thought for a moment, then replied:

'That's a very good idea, and I would love to do it, only unfortunately I'm completely illiterate.'

William kept such a straight face that for a moment Grant took him seriously.

Sophie admonished him:

'William, you shouldn't joke about things like that. It's unkind towards people who really are illiterate.'

'Sorry,' William acknowledged, 'I consider myself suitably chastised.'

He lifted his left hand and slapped it with his right, then

looked around the gathering, expecting a ripple of amusement to be forthcoming, but there was none. Indeed John Dyson, seated at two o'clock with his wife Pat at three, commented that his father had been illiterate, and that this had not prevented him from becoming a successful businessman.

William decided to concentrate on his meal and keep quiet for a while. He couldn't help feeling a little self-conscious now, a discomfort to which he was unaccustomed, being confident and outgoing by nature. He contemplated the circle individually. To his right Anita was now attempting to instil in Grant the passion for horse riding which she shared with Sophie and which had been the foundation of their friendship of several years. The Dysons and the Burkins were engrossed in conversation about the Middle East crisis, from which William was able to glean that John Dyson was a senior civil servant working for the Foreign Office. On the other side of the Burkins were a couple who had introduced themselves as Dr and Mrs King. William could just about make out that they were enquiring about local activities and facilities from the final members of the party, the Bennetts, who were positioned between them and Sophie. It transpired that Dr King had recently retired from his position of consultant in a hospital casualty department. Periodically William looked enquiringly towards Sophie, who seemed very subdued. She smiled uneasily in response to his glances. William couldn't help feeling that his own uncharacteristic behaviour was in some way connected with Sophie's malaise.

A snippet of the conversation between the Kings and the Bennetts caught William's attention:

'Yes, I knew him well. We were at college together,' Dr King was saying. 'He was a decent and thoroughly likeable man, and his achievements were quite remarkable. It's unthinkable that anyone should want to kill him.'

'We met him too,' added Henry Burkin, who had also picked up on the mention on Dr Walsingham.

'Yes, we have all enrolled at the Walton Foundation,'

Melissa Burkin explained. 'I think it's simply wonderful. Seventy or eighty years of life just are *not* enough. There are so many things I want to do, so many places I want to go, so many books I want to read.'

'That's right!' enthused Anita; the whole gathering was now party to this conversation. 'I think it's the most incredible thing that's ever happened. I'm going to be twenty-two for as long as I want to be.' William noticed that she was looking directly at Sophie, from which he inferred that she was hoping to influence her. Clearly they must have discussed the matter beforehand, he concluded, and it struck him that this might be the source of Sophie's last minute reluctance to attend the dinner party.

'What do you think, William?' Anita asked.

'Oh, I don't have any strong views either way. I'm not ready to think about something like that. When I'm older I'll give it some thought.'

Anita looked mystified. Sophie stared down at her now empty dinner plate, as if some form of miniature activity taking place on it was compelling her to watch. William, sensing the need to change the subject, remembered Sophie's earlier comment about Anita's wish to discuss his legal studies.

'Rabbits!' said Henry Burkin loudly and the patio doors opened, revealing a near dark but still pleasantly warm late summer's evening. Anyone who cared to take a stroll in the grounds to the rear of the house was invited to do so. Anita and Grant disappeared for a while, prompting a question in William's mind. Looking at Sophie, he raised his eyebrows; she understood and shook her head.

'More sake?' Melissa Burkin offered. William declined, explaining that he was driving.

Soft music could be heard: Randy Crawford was singing *One day I'll fly away.*

The Bennetts were telling the Kings that they were going on holiday early in the morning, and that they would have to go soon, as they did not want to repeat a recent experience of oversleeping and missing their flight.

Grant and Anita returned, and Anita called Sophie over to show her some photographs of her equestrian activities.

William was left with the Dysons and Henry Burkin.

'So what do you say to make the doors close?' William wanted to know.

'Bunnies!' said Burkin, and the doors obliged, causing some tittering among the observers. 'Why don't you give it a try?' he suggested.

'Rabbits!' said William; there was no response.

'Louder,' Burkin urged him, grinning.

William repeated the call in a raised voice, provoking curious looks from the other groups.

Henry Burkin chuckled and looked pleased with himself.

'It won't work for you, I'm afraid,' he explained. 'The system doesn't recognise your voice.'

Melissa Burkin, who had finished replenishing the wine glasses, joined them.

'Oh Henry, must you always tease our guests?' she admonished her husband.

'Rabbits!' cried Burkin defiantly, and the patio doors duly re-opened.

'Please excuse my husband!' Melissa entreated. Turning to William, she continued: 'Anita tells me you are intending to go to watch Sussex at Lord's next weekend.'

'Yes, that's right, it's the final of the one-day knockout.'

'Well, I know Henry's friend Jeremy would love to keep you company, if that's possible. He would have to meet you there, because he lives in Barnet, but we could help you make the necessary arrangements. I know it's a bit of a liberty to ask you. Henry would normally go with him, only my cousin is arriving from New York next Friday.'

Melissa broke off, realising she no longer had William's attention. Noticing that he was looking anxiously over her shoulder, she turned to see what was wrong.

Something was happening to Sophie.

'Excuse me,' said William, and he hurried off after her, catching up with her just after she made it through the doors onto the patio. Their presence triggered a mechanism which brightly illuminated the scene, revealing a dazzling handkerchief mopping the teardrops trickling down Sophie's cheeks. Puzzled eyes from within contemplated this scenario too; Anita in particular looked concerned. Sophie gazed back helplessly at the congregation inside. William, sensing her embarrassment, led her down the steps and across the lawn until they were away from the house. Spotting a bench near the trees, William guided Sophie to it and sat down beside her, his arm around her, tears moistening his shirt and collar.

'What? What is it?' he asked.

Sophie was struggling to speak. 'Hold on a minute,' she managed at last. She raised her head, wiped her tear-stained cheeks and blinked several times until William's face became visible.

'Has someone upset you?' he asked, unable to wait any longer.

'No, oh no, not at all.'

'What then?'

'You might not understand.'

'Try me.'

'Well,' she began hesitantly, 'it was the music.'

'The music? But that was lovely music.'

'No, it's not that the music itself upset me. You're right, Randy Crawford sings beautifully. It was what it reminded me of.'

'Ah, I see.' He paused momentarily. 'Your mother?' he asked softly.

'Yes. That song which was on just now... *Rainy night in Georgia*, that was what I was listening to when I took the call from the hospital. I had forgotten that until just then. Suddenly everything came flooding back.'

William passed one hand through Sophie's hair until it reached the back of her neck; gently he pulled her head towards him and cradled it under his chin.

'It's okay now,' he whispered.

'You understand?'

'Sure.'

'You don't think I'm strange?'

'Not at all.'

They sat silently for some moments.

'I had just come back from a driving lesson,' Sophie recounted. 'It hadn't gone very well, and I put my Randy Crawford CD on in order to relax. That song had just started when the phone rang.' She paused for a second, before adding:

'That's why I still haven't learnt to drive. Having another lesson would remind me of that day.'

'Oh, Sophie, poor you! I wish you had told me before. Listen, I'll help you learn to drive.'

'You will?'

'Yes, and by the next time you have a lesson, you'll be looking forward to it, because I'll make sure you enjoy it and you know what you're doing.'

Sophie looked up. A faint smile had returned to her face.

'Oh William, thank you.'

'It's okay.' He looked at her curiously. 'You sensed something was going to go wrong this evening, didn't you? How can you know something like that?'

'Oh I don't know anything, I just felt uncomfortable. I can't explain it. Maybe it *is* just coincidence. Or maybe because I think something's going to happen I make it happen.'

Sophie stood up. 'Come on, let's go back inside,' she said, taking him by the hand.

'Are you sure you're all right?'

'Yes I'm sure. Do I look reasonably presentable?'

William stood up and peered at her.

A solitary oak tree which stood a little closer to the house than the others obscured the light; William moved slightly aside so that Sophie's head was silhouetted against the gleam which still emanated from above the patio.

A split second later Sophie found herself tight up against the tree.

'Oh, William,' she purred.

Sophie closed her eyes and opened her mouth, but the anticipated passion did not materialise. She could tell William was close, because she could feel his breath on her forehead.

Opening her eyes she saw William's index finger, held vertically against pursed lips. Looking up slightly, she saw the fear in his eyes.

'Shush!'

His finger became a hand placed over her mouth, in case she screamed.

Then there was a loud bang from behind her, noisier than any firework – a short, crisp, crack accompanied by a flash of light.

Instantly she heard shouting and screaming, but this was silenced by a succession of explosive sounds, different from the first, recognisable even to Sophie's untrained ear as the sound of gunfire.

Then all went quiet, and Sophie and William remained where they were, statuesque, observing each other's terror at close quarters. Sophie prayed that the attackers would not choose to make their escape through the woods at the back of the house.

At last William dared to look round the tree, just in time to catch sight of a single dark figure disappearing round the side of the house.

William addressed Sophie in a hushed but emphatic voice:

'Stay there! Don't move! Wait for me to come back!'

Forgoing the protection afforded by the tree, William hurried towards the house, looking fearfully in the direction of the fleeing figure, just in case they returned. Uncertain as to whether there might be another intruder within, and filled with dread at the prospect of the scene he was about to behold, William approached the patio with caution. Smoke was billowing through the open doors.

Gingerly he entered the room. He came across the body of Henry Burkin, and beside him those of John and Pat Dyson.

They had caught the full force of the explosion, and William did not need to check to see that they were dead. Finding Melissa Burkin face downwards on the floor, however, he felt for a pulse and found one. Turning her over, he discovered that her white blouse was soaked with blood from a gunshot wound in her chest. She opened her eyes momentarily and mouthed something incomprehensible. For about a minute William stayed with her, holding her hand while she gasped and spluttered. Then her head fell back and consciousness slipped from her for the final time.

William stood up and stepped back, cursing his helplessness, wondering whether his intervention had made Melissa's passing more or less painful.

Turning, he could see through the clearing air that Grant was kneeling over Anita. The first to react to the sight of the grenade as it rolled across the floor, Grant had dived for cover behind the sofa and was miraculously unscathed. Crouching beside him, William looked at Anita, willing her to show signs of life. Grant let go of her hand, looked at William and shook his head.

'Thank God,' a voice from behind them could be heard to say. Dr King, spared by the timing of his answer to the call of nature, had returned to find his wife flat out on the floor. William went over to them. 'She's coming round,' the doctor assured him. Mrs. King had been knocked unconscious by the initial blast but had not been harmed by the bullets. 'She'll be all right,' Dr King affirmed.

Grant picked up Anita's mobile phone and dialled 999. Simultaneously a phone in an adjacent room could be heard ringing: it went unanswered until Henry Burkin's recorded message cut in – a now eerie reminder of the inventor's chirpiness. Mrs King sat up and began to make sense of her surroundings.

Sophie, unable to wait any longer, and beginning to fear for William's safety, was heading back towards the house. Her trepidation was eased when she saw William coming towards her. They met at the top of the patio steps and embraced.

Sophie's eyes asked the dreadful question. William, not knowing how to answer, began with the positive news:

'Grant and the Kings are okay.' Then, almost as an afterthought, he added: 'The Bennetts must have gone.'

Sophie's look became more pressing.

'Everyone else…'

William's voice tailed off; he did not need to finish the sentence.

Sophie buried her head on William's shoulder and began to sob.

Chapter 8

Lucky punched the air in jubilation as the putt which he had struck a little too firmly hit the back of the cup, popped up in the air for a moment, then dropped back into the hole.

'That's it then, Jimmy, I win two and one,' he chuckled, as they shook hands. 'Double or quits tomorrow?'

'No, this is getting out of my league,' said his golfing companion. 'I'll settle up when we get back to the clubhouse.'

'Shame,' said Lucky. 'It was just beginning to get interesting. Are you sure?'

'Yes, that's three defeats in three days you've given me. That's enough for me. In any case, I don't like going beyond ten grand.'

Lucky's grin became broader. The sum obviously meant a lot more to Jimmy than it did to him.

'Will you stop for a meal and a drink or three in the clubhouse?' he enquired.

Jimmy hesitated. 'I'll stay for a quick drink, but I won't eat. Carol's cooking a roast this evening.'

They set off in the direction of the clubhouse.

Lucky resumed the conversation:

'It's all right for you, having a meal waiting for you when you get home. I've got no chance of that at the moment.'

'How is Sophie today?'

'Oh, she's still in a world of her own. I don't know what to do about her.'

'It can't have been easy, Lucky, for a young woman to deal with something as awful as that.'

'I know it must have been shocking, but she's got to get over it.'

'Give her time. She had a narrow escape, you know.'

'Yes, it was a bloody good thing she was out the back.' He grinned at Jimmy, then added: 'That kind of luck runs in the family, you know.'

Jimmy took the opportunity to satisfy his curiosity:

'So why do they call you Lucky?'

'When I was a kid, I was a troublemaker, always up to no good. I wasn't much better after I grew up. I got involved with the wrong people, I guess. But I always got away with it, even when other people got caught. My dad said I should have been called Lucky, and I said I liked the name, so it stuck.'

They reached the clubhouse, and leaving their trolleys outside, went into the locker room. Jimmy wrote a cheque to cover Lucky's winnings and they went on into the bar. Flushed with success, Lucky bought drinks for Jimmy and himself, then offered to extend the round to the handful of golfers already congregated in the bar. A bearded man seated on a bar stool immediately to the right of Lucky took him up on the offer.

'You're Lucky Hanson, aren't you?'

'Sure am.'

'I'm Carl Furey. I work for the *Mid-Sussex Echo*. You play here regularly, don't you?'

'That's right, I'm here most days. I haven't seen you here before.'

'No, I've only just joined the club. Listen, I wrote the article in Tuesday's issue about last Saturday's tragic attack. I understand your daughter was involved.'

Lucky looked at him a little suspiciously.

'Yes, she was there, but she didn't see anything.'

'I know. I spoke to William Spencer. He didn't see much either. Look, I'll be straight with you. I was intending to do a follow-up article for next week's issue, focusing on the aftermath of the attack, looking at how the survivors were coming to terms with what happened.'

Lucky's suspicions were mounting.

'Well, you can't talk to Sophie. She's hardly speaking to anyone at the moment.'

'That's okay. In that case, I wouldn't want to trouble her. But I would be interested in hearing what you've got to say about it.'

Lucky looked at him closely.

'Did you come here just to see me?'

'Oh no, honestly, it's my day off. I've been playing a match. But I did know you were a member here, and I was hoping I might bump into you, and now I have.'

'So what do you want to know?'

'I would just like to ask you a few questions about how it has affected your family, what your reaction has been, what your feelings are towards the attackers…'

'I would kill them,' Lucky interrupted.

'Yes, quite,' Furey responded. He had the look of an angler who had just felt a tug at his line.

Lucky continued:

'I just hope that when they're caught they don't escape the chair just because some lawyer whinges about diminished responsibility or any of that twaddle.'

'So you agree with the reintroduction of the death penalty?'

'For those scumbags? You bet I do.'

'You think there's more than one killer, then?'

Lucky thought for a moment.

'I dunno. That dozy boyfriend of Sophie's isn't sure whether the bloke he saw just before the grenade went off was the same one he saw running away afterwards.'

Lucky gulped his beer before continuing:

'If you ask me, though, those damned protesters are responsible for this situation. I would have them all put away in some camp or something until they handed over the ones who did this.'

Furey's look betrayed both amusement and bewilderment.

'But the police aren't even convinced there's any connection with the protesters!'

'Oh yeah? What's the matter with them? Look, that doctor, what was his name?'

'Walsingham.'

'Yes, him. First someone shoots him. Then a week later a family who are all patients at his clinic are murdered. Are you trying to tell me that's just coincidence?'

Furey noticed that Lucky's beer glass was empty.

'Can I get you another?' he asked.

Imogen Spencer tapped lightly on the door of the bedroom, but there was no reply. She knocked again, slightly louder this time, but still there was no response. She turned the handle quietly, and opened the door slowly, until she was able to peer through the gap. All was still and silent; the curtains were drawn, but it was just possible to see strands of blonde hair nestling on the lilac coloured pillow. A forlorn face was hidden from the world – a world which had recently become an unwelcome sight each time the young eyes were forced to open. For a whole week now, Sophie's first thought each time she awoke was the same: it really happened. It wasn't a bad dream, or a quirk of her imagination: it was reality, showing its most macabre face.

One night there had been a heavy storm, and the first crash of thunder had struck just as Sophie had begun to succumb to her exhaustion. She sat bolt upright and relived the moment when the grenade had exploded, this time without William to smother her, without anyone to prevent her from screaming. Nor was there anyone to hear her cry out, her father's room being located right at the other end of the corridor.

William's mother waited a minute for signs of activity, but Sophie did not stir. The breakfast cereal packet which had been bought especially for her had long been put away in the cupboard, but Mrs Spencer had felt confident that Sophie would be down in time for lunch, and had cooked sufficient quantities of eggs, bacon, sausages and chips to cater for her visitor as well as her husband and son. Now it looked as though there was going to be a surplus.

Imogen closed the door and allowed her face to convey her concern to her son.

'At least she's sleeping,' William pointed out.

'Yes, but she needs to eat as well. We can't leave her there all afternoon. Give her another hour or so. If she doesn't come down by then I'll wake her up.'

Inside the bedroom, Sophie was vaguely aware that someone had opened and closed the door, and was becoming conscious of William's voice in the background. She remembered now that she had agreed to spend the weekend with the Spencers in the hope that a change of scenery and company would do her some good. She recalled that when her father had been late back from his golf match she had been persuaded to leave him a note explaining her whereabouts and hoped that he would not be cross.

Then Sophie remembered that today was the day that William had planned to watch the cricket. He had stayed at home to be with her, claiming that he didn't really feel like it anyway. She decided she ought to get up shortly. But first she had to run through what had happened in her mind once more, to attempt to come to terms with it, while the memory of Anita, her parents and the Dysons was still fresh. Sleep had rendered her imagination fertile again, and in her mind's eye various images of each of the victims vied for her attention. Henry Burkin was demonstrating a gadget which could empty your washing machine for you and then hang the clothes up to dry. It had a face which beamed at you and it could whistle or hum if you wanted. Anita waved in thanks as a Parcelforce driver stopped his van and waited for her to urge Peanut to overcome his fear of vehicles with loud engines.

And then, quite unexpectedly, Anita's face began to change, gaining in maturity but not losing its beauty, until Sophie beheld a different image, wonderful in its clarity. All at once a magical aroma delighted Sophie's nostrils, and a voice could be heard, oozing tenderness and relief…

'It's only me. Oh, thank goodness you're safe, my child… and William too. I know, I know. It's all right now.'

'Mum, what are you doing here?'

'I'm here for you, to help you. I'm just so grateful you weren't hurt, and you didn't see too much either, did you? And William was so brave, going back in the house, not knowing who might have been in there waiting for him, trying to help poor Melissa.'

'We were just lucky we were outside. If it had not been for that song…'

'I know, my dear. It was me that made them play it. I knew what it would do to you. I'm sorry, but I had to do it. I had to get you out of that room.'

'So that was you? I thought it was too much of a coincidence that the same song which reminded me of the day you died had caused something to happen which saved our lives.'

The face which Sophie's mind was entertaining was radiant now, as though illuminated by an invisible halo. Tranquillised by the state of semi-consciousness which had enveloped her, Sophie nevertheless accepted the premise that her mother was with her, looking after her, keeping watch over her like a guardian angel.

'You haven't been practising, have you my dear? You should, you know. It will do you good. Imogen would love to hear you play, I know she would.'

'Okay, I'll play for her, and for you, of course.'

'Play something cheerful.'

'I will. And then I'll go home and see how Dad is.'

'Ah, your father! I doubt whether he's got a clue how you feel!'

'What should I do about him?'

'Be patient, my child. He can't help the way he is.'

'Should I go home yet?'

'No, not if you're not ready yet. It will do you good to stay here. William's mother is such a sweet, caring soul. Spend some time with her and get to know her better. You'll be glad you did.'

Something must have disturbed Sophie, because the image began to flicker, the way a television picture does when a fault occurs.

'Don't go yet, Mum.'

'It's not me; it's you who must go. Bye, my child. Stay safe.'

The bedroom door opened, and Sophie realised that it was the knocking which had roused her.

She sat upright, and peered through the half light until she realised it was William who was standing in the doorway, his boyish face pointed enquiringly toward her.

'Your dad's on the phone. He wants to know when you're coming home.'

Sophie couldn't help feeling irritated. As usual, her father wanted to know the information which was relevant to his needs – not how she was feeling, what she had been doing, whether she was any better, but when she would be there again to listen to his gloating about how he had trounced Jimmy Whatshisname at golf and then at snooker, or to sympathise about the fact that those useless mechanics still hadn't got Sunday's car running smoothly, or to check he had remembered his dental appointment.

'My mum says you are to stay as long as you want,' William added.

'Tell him I'll be back on Monday or Tuesday,' Sophie declared at length.

Then she realised William was carrying a cordless phone in his right hand; she raised her eyes to the ceiling before reaching out for the receiver.

'Are you sure you'll be all right?' William asked as he returned to his father's sports car, having left Sophie's suitcase at the top of the steps to *Paradise*. Sophie nodded, leaned across and gave him a long, lingering kiss, a kiss which said 'thank you', 'I love you' and 'I need you' all at once, more effectively than words ever could.

Sophie skipped up the steps as if to demonstrate that she had rediscovered her usual vitality. She turned, waved briefly and vigorously, and disappeared inside. In an instant William was gone, bound for his friend Trevor's house en route to Brighton for the re-arranged kite surfing trip.

Sophie paused to gather up the day's post, as well as *The*

Independent and the local paper, on top of which the assortment of envelopes had landed. She took the bundle through to the kitchen, placed it on the worktop and set about making herself a cup of coffee. She was glad that she had the whole of *Paradise* to herself for a while. Hopefully her father would not return until the evening, and would be basking in the glory of his latest golfing triumph. He would have had a few drinks and a meal; he would not be feeling argumentative and all would be well. She wondered whether he would notice how much better she looked, at least so William and his family had repeatedly assured her. She had played the piano to Imogen, as her mother had suggested, and this had evoked such a rapturous reception that she had performed again, both on Sunday and Monday, and had led the chorus of 'Happy Birthday' to William's father, Dudley, on Monday evening.

As she watched the kettle boil Sophie recalled the moment on Sunday afternoon when William had pointed out, with a wink, that his parents had gone for a walk and that they had the house to themselves for a while. Standing over her as she sat on the piano stool, his hand had strayed down from her shoulder onto her breast, probing for a response which was not forthcoming. She had told him apologetically that she was not ready for that yet and he had understood. Sophie had even toyed with the idea of confiding in William about the appearance of her mother, which had such an uplifting effect on her, but she had refrained because she didn't feel able to explain something she didn't altogether understand herself. Sophie had never told anyone about these experiences, which had previously taken place solely at her mother's grave, after considerable mental effort on her part. She had understood them as being the product of her own exceptionally vivid imagination. On this occasion the image of her mother had appeared unexpectedly, and she felt unsure whether it might have been some sort of visitation. Or perhaps she had been dosing more deeply than she had realised and had been dreaming.

Sophie took her coffee through to the lounge, and then returned for the pile of correspondence. She realised that she had lost track of the date, and checked *The Independent:* Tuesday 8th September 2009. Ten days had elapsed since the awful day. The police were no closer to knowing who was responsible. In the immediate aftermath of the attack, there had been prominent reports in the national press, which Sophie had tried to avoid as much as possible. Now, however, the incident was old news and she was able to scan *The Independent* without coming across any reference to it. She felt slightly greater trepidation when she turned her attention to the *Mid-Sussex Echo*. It was possible that this week's edition would wish to fill in details which were unavailable the previous week. It was possible…her gaze fell on a reference on the front page to an article within: 'Horsham man tells of daughter's terrorist trauma'. Surely not, she thought. Sophie knew her father had a low opinion of journalists. A number of them had tried to speak to her in the days which had followed the attack and he had sent them all packing. She turned to page four…and there indeed was Lucky, photographed in colour outside a building she recognised as the golf course clubhouse, looking flushed with anger, a hostile glare in his eyes.

The article began with her father's recollection of the moment when Sophie had returned from the deadly dinner party after spending the early hours of the morning giving statements to the police. Lucky explained that he had learned what had happened from William because his daughter was too upset to go over it again. He went on to describe how he was trying to get her to put the incident behind her and get on with her life. Thankfully there was little mention of her feelings or reactions. However, what really troubled Sophie was the evidence of the extent of her father's contempt. Criticising the police for not having brought the attackers to justice, Lucky condemned those protesting against the Walton Foundation as the scum of the earth, adding that if he had his way he would stick the murderers in a giant microwave.

Sophie's strained expression as she tossed the paper aside told of her dismay, her vexation and her bewilderment. She collected her thoughts. Her first reaction was one of anger that her father had spoken to the reporter without her consent; moreover she did not take kindly to his remarks about the protesters. However these feelings had been superseded by her anxiety about the reaction of the attackers if the report came to their attention. Sophie was fearful for her father's safety following the massacre at the Burkin's house. His comments in the article had served only to exacerbate her fears.

Returning to the kitchen Sophie replenished her coffee cup. Suddenly she wished she had decided to stay at William's house. She had consented to go home because she knew her father needed her, or rather he needed *somebody* there, simply because he hated being alone. Also she felt duty-bound to keep an eye on him, knowing how irrational he could be. And now he had caused her more distress without even being there. With a sigh, she went back to the lounge and took one more look at the article, as if to check that her eyes had not deceived her. Wishing to take her mind off the matter for a while, she thumbed through the collection of mainly white envelopes she had retrieved from the hall. There was an invitation to join a book club (special offer inside); then there was the phone bill, and an update regarding her adoptive 'Granny' in Africa, which she put to one side to read properly later. And then there was a brown envelope which curiously did not have a stamp on it. She looked to see whether it was for her or for her father, but then she realised it had not even been addressed. In fact, she noticed, it hadn't even been sealed. She held it up and allowed the contents to tip out. A single sheet of plain, white, paper floated down to the floor, landing face downwards.

Obviously someone had written them a note, Sophie concluded. Puzzled, she stooped to pick it up, and started to read it.

It was a short note. It had been written using a red biro.

All the letters were capitals. A stencil had been used so that there could be no question of identifying the author by examining the handwriting. Although there were only three words, it contained a grammatical irregularity which might have suggested to an attentive observer that the writer lacked the sophistication required to pay heed to the finer points of the English language. This fact, however, was lost on Sophie, for whom the implications of the content of the note were infinitely more significant. The note said simply: HANSON YOUR NEXT.

Chapter 9

As Lucky picked up the phone and dialled the number he looked out of the window, across the front lawn and towards the chestnut trees. A white squirrel scampered along one of the branches, which buckled slightly, then shook as the rodent leapt across to another tree. A prickly green ball fell to the ground, cracking open on impact to reveal the first conker of the season.

'Hello, yes, is Sophie there?'

'Hold on,' replied Dudley Spencer.

Lucky tapped the receiver impatiently while he waited for his daughter to come to the phone.

'Sophie,' he was able to say at last. 'Listen, I've found someone. He's free to start immediately. He's moving in tomorrow morning. I'm going to send him round in the afternoon to pick you up.'

'I can't come home just like that, Dad. I've arranged with all my pupils for the rest of the week to come here for their lessons. Anyway, I think we should give him at least a week to settle in to make sure he stays, otherwise I'm not stopping. And I can't possibly mess Imogen and Dudley about. They've been very kind and understanding…'

'Don't keep on about how bloody wonderful they are. It's really getting on my nerves.'

'Well, give them some credit. Imogen understands so well what I've been through. She's so like Mum…'

'Then she ought to be telling you that you belong here at a time like this. Look, I've met all your bloody demands. I've had security cameras put in all over the estate, I've grovelled to those pig-faced reporters until they included that ridiculous apology you made me write, and I've hired a bodyguard who's prepared to live here. Have you any idea how much that's costing me? It's down to you to do your bit and get yourself back here pretty damn quick. I hope I'm getting through to you, Sophie. I've moved heaven and earth for you, and don't you forget it. Okay?'

'Look, Dad, you ought to know by now that if I say I'll do something then I will. If this chap stays, then I'll come back at the weekend. It's just not practicable before that. Anyway, please try to be civil and considerate to him, for your own sake.' She paused for a moment; Lucky sighed in exasperation. 'Listen, I'm very glad you've found someone, but it's important you're able to get on with him, especially as you're going to be spending so much time with him. What's he like, anyway?'

'He's about thirty, and he's called Phil. He doesn't say very much, but he seems as though he's got his wits about him.'

'Good. And is he going to go with you when you play golf?'

'Yes, he's a golfer himself, so he's either going to play or caddie for me. The more often we go the better, he said.'

'Did you put him in the picture about what has happened?'

'Of course.'

'What did he say?'

'He agrees that it's probably some crackpot from the anti-Walton Foundation mob who read the article and wants to put the wind up me.'

'Well, I hope he's going to take it seriously, anyway.'

'Oh yeah, don't worry, I'm going to make sure he keeps his eyes peeled.'

'All right, Dad. I have to go. I've got to give a lesson in a few minutes. Ring me tomorrow night and let me know how things are going.'

'Things will be fine, don't worry. So you can tell your pupils their lessons will be in the usual place next week.'

'Look, I'll tell them they will be unless they hear otherwise. Okay?'

'I suppose so. Bye for now.'

'Bye, Dad.'

Sophie had mixed feelings as she gave the cordless phone back to Dudley. She couldn't help feeling anxious about going back to *Paradise*, on the one hand because she was conscious of the threat to their safety. on the other because she was still not looking forward to trying to live with her father again. And she would miss the comfort and solace that William and his family had brought her. However she felt uneasy that she had now been staying with them for over two weeks, and did not want to take advantage of their hospitality. She had decided she would offer to take them out for a meal to thank them for their kindness.

The moment Sophie read the threatening note she had called a taxi and headed for the golf course. In the pro shop she had asked what time her father had begun his round and ascertained roughly whereabouts on the course he was likely to be. She then threaded her way through the incoming parties of golfers, dodging their shots and disdainful looks until she caught up with him on the fifteenth tee. Lucky spotted her just before it was his turn to play and completely fluffed his tee shot. His irritation was aggravated when she explained the reason for tracking him down. She showed him the note, and he examined it for a few seconds before cursing those concerned in the most foul and abusive language she had ever heard him use. The three golfers with him gathered round, asked questions and offered their opinions. One of them dismissed the note with a shake of the head: 'It wouldn't make sense, if they were serious about bumping you off, to warn you first, would it? They would just be making life more difficult for themselves, wouldn't they?'

'You're right, Frank,' Lucky concluded. 'Some crazy prat is trying to put the frighteners on me. Well, they've got the wrong person. I don't scare that easily.' And with that he screwed the note up into a ball, tossed it in the air, and kicked it into the thick rough which lined the fifteenth fairway. 'Come on, let's get on with the game,' he said to the others. They returned their clubs to their bags and set off, leaving Sophie, open-mouthed and speechless, angrier and more distraught than she had been before she arrived. 'See you in the clubhouse,' Lucky called to her over his shoulder. Not wishing them to see how upset she was, Sophie waited for them to play their second shots before following them up the fairway. Halfway along the hole she realised that she ought to retrieve the note. If her father wasn't prepared to deal with the situation, then she was, and she would begin by reporting the matter to the police. She turned and began to walk back towards the tee. A loud shout coming from the direction in which she was walking startled her and she froze. Something landed right in front of her, and then whistled past her ear, frightening her again. Turning, she saw the small, white, round object bouncing a couple more times before rolling into a bunker.

'This is a golf course, you idiot!' shouted the lone golfer who had waited until she was out of range before preparing to play his shot, only to discover to his horror that she had turned back and was walking directly into the path his ball was taking. Sophie allowed the golfer to pass before resuming her quest. As the man approached he looked towards her and was about to rebuke her again, but then he noticed how distressed she looked and thought better of it.

Finding the note immediately, Sophie unravelled it carefully and made her way back to the clubhouse, keeping her distance from her father's party so that she could concentrate on considering what to do. From the phone in the entrance she tried calling William on his mobile, but it was switched off: presumably he was already in the sea. So she rang his home number instead, and Imogen answered. 'Stay where you are, I'll come and get you,' she assured Sophie.

Lucky was just arriving at the final green when he noticed Sophie getting into a small blue car driven by a woman he vaguely recognised but couldn't quite place. Imogen drove back to *Paradise* where they retrieved the suitcase which Sophie had not had time to unpack and helped her gather together enough things to last her for a much longer stay. They worked quickly, sensing each other's disquiet at being alone in the mansion, unsure whether they were entirely safe, their minds entertaining the horrendous possibility, remote but nonetheless real, of an attack at any moment.

'Don't you think we should ring the police from here?' Sophie asked Imogen, as they were about to leave.

Imogen shook her head. 'Not if you're sure your dad will stay in the clubhouse.'

'He always does.'

'Right, he'll be safe enough over there. Let's ring them when we get to mine.'

Sophie remembered that her pupils would be resuming their lessons the following week. Imogen thought for a moment, and then suggested re-routing them to her house. The piano was perfectly adequate, was it not? So Sophie fetched her address book and the music scores she required and they were on their way to the sanctuary of the Spencers' home.

The police had examined the note and compared it to the typewritten one sent to Dr Walsingham prior to his murder. The note received by the scientist had been longer and had arrived through the post, and larger paper had been used. They concluded that it was impossible to draw any firm conclusions one way or the other as to whether they were from the same source, or whether there was a genuine threat, but advised that it was best to take no chances. That evening Sophie, William, Dudley and Imogen discussed the matter at length. Taking the advice of the police about increasing security precautions, they drew up a list of conditions which Lucky would have to meet before Sophie should consider returning home. Imogen re-iterated that she could remain with them for as long as she wanted.

And so she had stayed, in a room of her own, just down the corridor from William's bedroom. The Spencers had declined any contribution towards the running expenses or for the food. William had been very sympathetic, especially in view of the fact that she had continued to refuse his advances. 'It's not you,' she assured him. 'I'm still grieving. I just don't feel right about enjoying myself at the moment.' Sophie explained that traumatic experiences affect women in different ways from men. William accepted this; however she had sensed his mounting frustration, and felt guilty. More than once, while they were out together, she had noticed other women catching his eye. She felt uncomfortable, even threatened, but was unable to make an issue of it. After all, it was only natural, was it not? So she overlooked these indiscretions, and focused on the supportiveness and companionship which William had offered unstintingly.

In a week's time William would be flying to America, bound for the experience of a lifetime. How she wished it could have taken place some other time, not while she was trying to get over the shock of the massacre while at the same time facing up to the anxiety which the threatening note had instilled in her. If only the attackers had been apprehended... but the police were none the wiser. If only there were some way of deferring the trip... but she knew that the Spencers had spent a vast amount of money on William's space holiday, and would lose most of it if he cancelled his trip at the last moment. After their kindness to her, she could not bring herself to ask them to consider that option. There was no alternative; she would simply have to do without him for four weeks. Anyway, she would have to get used to seeing less of him, because he would be starting work shortly after his return, and during the week he would be renting an apartment in the Barbican from his uncle.

Sophie passed on the news of her father's appointment of a bodyguard to Dudley and Imogen; William was playing squash with Trevor at the time. She was touched by their response. They said they were glad, and tried to look pleased, but she sensed their disappointment at the implication that she would be returning home.

'Couldn't you stay until after William flies out on Tuesday?' Imogen asked.

'I would like to,' Sophie replied, 'but I've just told Dad that I'll be back at the weekend. He'll be really cheesed off if I'm not.'

'Surely he would realise that you would want to spend just a couple more days with William when you won't be seeing him at all for a month?'

Sophie struggled to explain:

'My dad can be very demanding. If he thinks for a moment that I'm not going to honour our agreement he might go and do something stupid.'

'Like what?'

'Like...I don't know...getting rid of the bodyguard, or driving round here at ninety miles per hour and having an accident.'

Imogen looked at her intently, a combination of bewilderment and exasperation about her.

'You don't think much of my dad, do you?' Sophie asked.

'It's not that,' Imogen assured her. 'It's just that I think you've got to be more assertive with him.' She paused, before continuing: 'Otherwise how will you ever have a life of your own?'

Sophie said nothing, but her expression indicated that she accepted the point. Imogen's remarks were a painful reminder of an uncomfortable aspect of Sophie's reality.

They agreed a compromise: Sophie would go home on Sunday, but would return on Monday evening for a farewell meal for William, and she would leave herself the option of staying the night and going with him to Gatwick airport early the next morning.

The remainder of the week shot by. William had left a lot to the last minute, and much of the time was spent ensuring that he was adequately prepared for his trip. Sophie tried to show interest and be helpful, but it seemed that everywhere around her there were indications of his imminent departure.

On several occasions she had to turn away from him in order to hide the fact that tears were forming in her eyes, and more than once she had to stop herself from burying her head in his chest, throwing her arms around him and imploring him not to go. She knew how excited he had been about this adventure ever since his parents had told him they would finance it, and she persistently told herself it would not be fair of her to spoil it for him.

Saturday arrived, and as Sophie awoke she could not help feeling downhearted. It was to be her last full day with William for a month. At the breakfast table Imogen, sensing her mood, suggested very pointedly to her son that it would be a lovely day for the couple to visit a country estate and to take a stroll in the gardens. Dudley proposed Leonardslee, adding that William could use the MG if he wanted. So that afternoon they journeyed to the other side of Horsham: William had it firmly in mind that his objective was to console Sophie. Imogen had tipped him off that there were some wallabies in the grounds – including some beautiful albinos – and that he should make sure Sophie saw them. Indeed there was a field full of the creatures, and among them was a solitary white one, which from a distance Sophie initially mistook for a large cat. The sight of these delightful animals, and especially the dazzling brilliance of the one that stood out, gave Sophie a moment to cherish, and William observed a smile broader than any she had given him for a while.

The gardens, which were set around seven small lakes, were full of colour. There were maple trees, adorned with red, russet and gold leaves, Somehow, however, the ambiance did not seem to have the desired effect, and as they travelled back to Rusper Sophie was struggling to raise her spirits. Partly it was because the gardens were exhibiting the mellowness which confirmed the onset of autumn, whereas Sophie relished the abundance of daylight and warmth which summertime offered. Also it was the fact that Leonardslee was situated on the same side of Horsham as *Paradise* and the journey was therefore an unwelcome reminder of what lay in store for her the next day. Furthermore she had found that Saturday had become the most difficult day of the week ever since the ordeal which had marked the start of her malaise exactly four weeks ago. Finally the thought that William's adventure might involve even a slight element of danger was unbearable to her. Although she had not experienced any sense of foreboding about the trip, she did not feel she could rule out the possibility that the unthinkable might happen to William somewhere in the vast, unseen wilderness about which she knew so little.

It was this concern which preoccupied her that night, preventing her from sleeping. She was also becoming conscious of a renewed craving to be physically close to William. How ironic, she reflected, that her desire for intimacy was returning just as he was about to leave. If only he knew how much she wanted him to stay. Despite her reluctance to tell him directly how she felt, Sophie had hoped that William would realise how distressing the prospect of their imminent separation was to her, perhaps even that he might feel likewise. She would have understood if he had thought that it would be unfair on his parents to squander the opportunity they had created for him at such expense. She would have been heartened if he had professed to having mixed feelings about being committed to going on the trip. What troubled her was that William had shown nothing but enthusiasm for this adventure, and was too excited to feel any apprehension about the matter of whether or not it was entirely safe. Moreover he seemed to have put the memory of *that evening* firmly behind him in a way which Sophie had hardly begun to do. For the first time in several years, Sophie found herself forced to ask whether they really were compatible as partners.

This was an uncomfortable thought to consider in the middle of a restless night, and she preferred to suppress the question rather than to contemplate it. After all, she reasoned, her unresponsiveness towards him during her stay must have left him feeling lukewarm about their relationship, and it was understandable that he should have focused instead on his dream holiday. Perhaps he just needed assurance that she still wanted to be with him…

Sophie tiptoed along the corridor, not wishing to make any sound which might disturb William's parents, whose bedroom was almost directly above her. She turned the handle and pushed the door to William's room until it was slightly ajar, then peered into the gloom. He did not stir. She entered the room and closed the door carefully behind her, then crept towards his bed. For a moment she wondered how to wake him without startling him: a touch, a whisper or a kiss? He was lying with his back to her, his face towards the window; the curtains had been drawn carelessly allowing a chink of light to filter through the gap in the middle. Eventually Sophie plucked up the courage to sit slowly down on the side of his bed, all the while prepared to hush him if he awoke with a start.

Still he did not move an inch. How could anyone sleep so soundly, she wondered? Gently she placed her right hand on his upper arm, and then moved it round onto his chest, spreading her fingers out amidst the little clump of hairs which nestled over his breastbone. She could feel the steady rise and fall of his torso and took comfort from this manifestation of well-being. Sophie moved her hand slightly, probing for the heartbeat, hoping that it might start to quicken as William became conscious of her proximity. However she was unable to make the connection and abandoned her quest.

Emboldened by a growing conviction that she was worrying unnecessarily about alarming him, she elected to lie in readiness beside him. Lifting the bedclothes, she slipped her legs underneath and wriggled into a horizontal position, her body shape mirroring his, her front against his back. Sooner or later he had to realise she was there, she concluded. So they lay there motionless, Sophie beginning to slip into semi-consciousness, William curiously unaware that his single bed was being treated as though it were a double.

Just as Sophie was on the verge of succumbing to her drowsiness, William twisted onto his back, and his head turned towards her, his nose coming to rest on the pillow right by her forehead. She moved slightly so that she could look into his eyes, but they remained closed.

'William,' she whispered.

'Hmm?' came the uncomprehending reply. For a moment one eye partially opened, but immediately shut again as if it had dismissed what it had seen as unreal or unwelcome. It was then Sophie remembered that he had drunk quite a few glasses of wine with the previous evening's meal.

'I wish you didn't have to go,' she said slowly, sorrowfully, as though making a confession.

There was no response. William had returned to his slumbers, and her words went unheeded.

Just before nine o'clock there was a soft tap on William's bedroom door. A few seconds later Imogen entered the room, carrying a tray which had two cups on. She knew that if her son was still asleep she would be able to cross the room, put his coffee on the bedside table, and draw back the curtains without disturbing him. Within a few minutes he would wake up, his mind somehow stimulated into activity by the aroma of the caffeine. In the meantime Imogen would have taken the cup of tea on to Sophie's room. The latter would usually be alert enough for them to hold a brief conversation; each would ask the other how well they had slept, or they would discuss the weather.

Imogen had already put the coffee cup down before she noticed anything different about this morning. She stood motionless for a moment, contemplating the scene. There was something rather touching about the way the two bodies were cramped into a space intended for one. She remembered, with a smile, her own courtship days and the first time she had visited Dudley in his bed-sit in Norwich. She wondered what to do about the drinks. Neither William nor Sophie had sensed her presence. Would they be embarrassed if they knew she had seen them in bed together? There was no point in carrying the cup of tea along to Sophie's room; they would still know she had come in. She would either have to take William's cup away again, and come back later, or else leave them both there. Imogen dithered for a moment longer, then arrived at a conclusion. She didn't care if they knew she had seen them. Indeed, she *wanted* them to know. Imogen was coming to think of Sophie as one of the family, and she was eager for them to know that she felt they belonged together. It occurred to Imogen that here was an opportunity for her to communicate this in the subtlest of ways. So she placed the teacup neatly beside the cup of coffee, leaving the handles almost touching, and smiled to herself as she quietly left the room.

Chapter 10

'She's just coming,' said Imogen, forcing herself to smile. 'Did you manage to find us all right?' she enquired through the open window on the driver's side of the car.

'Yes, thanks, it was no trouble,' he replied, confirming her impression that he spoke with a northern accent.

William came out of the front door, carrying a suitcase. The man opened the car door and helped him put it in the boot.

'You must be Phil,' William observed.

'Yes.'

'I'm William.' He held out his right hand and after a moment the man offered his in response. William noted that he seemed surprised at this proffer of acquaintance. He also noticed the man's imposing height. William was not short, but the top of his head failed to reach the man's shoulder.

'Sophie's boyfriend,' William explained.

The man nodded, as if to imply that he had already worked that out.

'So how's Mr. Hanson?' William asked, grinning mischievously. He was sure that the man would have realised that Lucky was a hard person to get on with – everybody knew that. Would he feel at liberty to admit it to him, or would he be on his guard in case something he said was passed on to his new employer?

'He's fine,' Phil replied earnestly.

'Good!' William enthused, a little taken aback. Surely the man didn't mean it?

'I'll just go and see where Sophie's got to,' he went on. Phil got back in the car. Imogen followed William to the front door, where they came across Sophie, who was just emerging, followed by Dudley.

Sophie thanked them profusely for their kindness; there were hugs and kisses, and reminders that they would see each other again tomorrow evening. It had suddenly begun to rain, and Sophie persuaded them that there was no need to get wet. She hurried out and round to the passenger side of the car, pausing momentarily for a final wave. Sophie went to open the front door of the vehicle, and then wondered whether this was appropriate. On the one hand the bodyguard was going to be living in *Paradise,* and it would be better to get to know him and make him feel at ease with her. On the other hand he was an employee of her father, and had come to fetch her because he was acting on his instruction. It was more like hiring a taxi, and her mother had taught her always to sit in the back whenever she took a taxi. She noticed a book and a newspaper on the front passenger seat, and made up her mind to get in the back.

'Hello,' she said as she sat down, 'I'm Sophie.'

'Good afternoon, miss. My name's Todd.'

Sophie puzzled for a moment, checking her memory, before replying:

'Oh, that's strange. My dad told me you were called Phil.'

The man turned the key in the ignition.

'Yes, that's right, Phil Todd. Most people just call me Todd.'

'What do you prefer to be called?'

'I don't mind.'

'Then I'll call you Phil.'

'Okay.'

As he set the vehicle in motion, Sophie caught a glimpse of his face for the first time in the interior mirror. He shared her eye colour, but his skin was darker and his nose flatter. He had close-cropped, brown hair. His expression was serious and rather intense, and he gave the impression that concentration on the task in hand came naturally to him. She could tell he must be tall from the proximity of his head to the roof of the vehicle. Somehow he *looked* like a bodyguard, a fact which Sophie found very reassuring. She wanted to put her mind at rest as to how he had been getting on with her father. Presumably things weren't too bad; after all he had lasted four days. She decided to make subtle enquiries.

'I hear you've been playing golf with Dad.'

'Yes, every day so far.'

'And can you beat him?'

'I won yesterday. We're fairly evenly matched.'

'You don't find him too competitive?'

'No, it's okay. I'm the same.'

'And you're enjoying it?'

'Yes, it's a great course.'

Although the implications of the outcome of her initial enquiry were encouraging, they were tempered by the thought that Phil might be compromising his effectiveness as a bodyguard if he was too taken up with playing golf. As though anticipating her misgivings, Phil continued:

'It's got a first class security system. I checked that out on Wednesday morning, before we went over there. The course was designed to enable very high-profile people to play there, so they have taken extra precautions. There's no way anyone could get on the course with a weapon. They even scan visitors' golf clubs to make sure they are genuine.'

Sophie was impressed:

'So you think Dad is completely safe when he's out there?'

Phil thought for a second.

'The only possibility would be an attack from the air. But I think it's extremely unlikely that these people would have the resources to attempt that. We're not dealing with some vast terrorist network, here, just one or two warped individuals. Still, I keep my eyes peeled just in case.'

He glanced in the mirror and noted the trace of anxiety that this new suggestion had brought to her face.

'Don't worry; the course is in the middle of a forest. At the slightest hint of danger, I would have him under the cover of the trees in no time.'

Sophie was quiet for a while, contemplating the way her life had changed over the past month. She remembered how content she had felt during the heatwave, which had spanned much of July and August, and wondered if she would ever feel so carefree again. Would she feel at ease walking into Copsale village now, or would she be looking warily at every unfamiliar vehicle or passer-by she came across in case they were on their way to *Paradise* with murderous intentions? How would she cope with being alone in the mansion? Would she be able to give her pupils her undivided attention, or would she be looking anxiously out of the window in case there were intruders in the grounds? In fact, should she not be warning the parents that there was no guarantee that the children were safe inside *Paradise*? She gave this last question considerable thought, and concluded that she ought indeed to write to them and explain the position, even if it meant risking losing some of her pupils.

Sophie decided to take her mind off these gloomy thoughts. She chatted to Phil, satisfying her curiosity about his background. She discovered he was a very strong swimmer, and had come close to qualifying for the Olympics as a youngster. He had worked as a lifeguard in a swimming pool, and as a gym instructor, before training as a bodyguard. He had protected politicians and diplomats on visits to dangerous foreign countries and was widely travelled: however he had been wishing for some time to be able to work exclusively in his home country and could not believe his good fortune when her father had offered him this position. All his pastimes were catered for: as well as the regular golfing trips, he had been told he could use the swimming pools (he had already been in the outdoor pool twice) and had discovered there was a very well equipped, newly built gym near Billingshurst. Sophie was glad to hear that he was satisfied with the room he had been given. Altogether, he seemed quite content, which was a considerable relief to her.

They were almost back in *Paradise*, and Sophie could not help feeling a little apprehensive.

'What do you think of the new security system my father has had installed?' she asked Phil.

'It's excellent,' he replied unhesitatingly. 'The cameras would pick up anyone attempting to enter the grounds by any means other than the main entrance and immediately trigger an alarm which could be heard everywhere on the estate. The police would be informed automatically. They would even be able to tell exactly where the problem was, and so would we. It works just as well in the dark as it does in daylight. If the alarm goes off every door and window in the mansion locks immediately, but if you happened to be outside you would be able to override this for long enough to enable you to get back inside. And we've altered the setting of the security system at the main entrance so that it only lets your dad's cars or mine through automatically, just in case an attacker hijacked a visitor's vehicle. It means we'll have to look at the screens in the hall before letting anyone else in, but I'm afraid that can't be helped. The scanners would detect anyone hiding in the back of the vehicle, or the boot of a car. Basically, I reckon the system is foolproof, and you should feel quite safe here.'

His conclusion coincided with their arrival at the gates to *Paradise*. It all sounded very convincing. Clearly a lot of thought had gone into the revision of the security features. '*You should feel quite safe here.*' She repeated Phil's final words in her mind, with the intention of being able to recall them on demand should any doubt arise.

Phil stopped the car at the bottom of the steps and went round to the boot. Sophie watched as he lifted the suitcase effortlessly and carried it up to the front door. As she followed him in Sophie noticed the revolver, tucked into a holster on his right side and felt a shudder. William had told her that recent legislation had permitted bodyguards who had undergone specific training and obtained a special licence to carry firearms, but only where a judge had given consent on the grounds that there was a known risk to the client. The sight of Phil's gun was another reminder of their newfound vulnerability. Sophie wondered whether he had ever had cause to use it, and decided she would prefer to remain ignorant of the answer to that question.

The hallway was empty.

'Where's Dad?' she asked.

'He's still up at the golf course. He wants me to go back for him after I've dropped you off.'

Sophie shook her head, and struggled to suppress her reaction. After all the fuss her father had made to get her to come back, he couldn't even manage to be there to welcome her. And what was more he expected her to wait there on her own the moment she arrived. For a moment she toyed with the idea of asking Phil to take her straight back to the Spencers' house, but concluded that if she didn't go through with her decision to come home now she might never be able to do it. So she calmed herself, and said simply: 'I'll come with you.'

'Okay,' said Phil, and for the first time she caught a glimpse of his shy smile.

'Five, four, three, two, one, blast-off!' cried Timmy Spencer, and the spacecraft took off from its launch pad on the dining room table. It rose in his hand until it reached the maximum height attainable by a model rocket when held aloft by a six-year-old standing on a chair. Its ascent was accompanied by sounds of 'Whoosh!' and 'Vroom!' On reaching the pinnacle of its orbit it began to duck and dive. At one point it nearly collided with Sophie's head.

Janet Spencer was becoming concerned that her son was irritating the other members of the dinner party.

'Come on, it's time we took you home to bed!' she intervened, lifting the little boy down and placing him on the floor. Timmy seized the opportunity to take the spacecraft on a voyage of exploration around the rooms on the ground floor of the Spencers' home. As well as the sounds of the rocket's engines there were imaginary conversations between the astronauts and "ground control". These were loud enough to filter through to the dining room, causing some mirth among the family. Sophie, however, did not laugh, managing at best an uneasy smile.

The unexpected visit of William's elder brother Toby had transformed the intimate atmosphere of the gathering and deprived her of the chance to have a heart-to-heart chat with her boyfriend before he left. Sophie knew she could have counted on Imogen and Dudley to have an early night in order to leave the couple to spend some time alone together at the end of the evening. Toby and his family's arrival just as they were finishing their meals had initially seemed unlikely to deny them this opportunity. She was confident that they would not keep young Timmy out too late, and Phil was not due to pick her up until eleven o'clock. However as the evening wore on it had become obvious that they were in no hurry to get home. And far from showing signs of fatigue Timmy had sprung to life after darkness had fallen.

Eventually Janet succeeded in retrieving her son from his flights of fantasy, and her husband from his lengthy conversation with William. It was a mild, dry night, affording the opportunity for a protracted farewell process. Finally their car took a left turn at the bottom of the drive and disappeared along the country lane towards Crawley.

Sophie checked her watch: it was ten to eleven, even later than she had realised. She could sense the tears welling up inside her and the lump forming in her throat. It had been a very trying couple of days. She had felt compelled to keep her dismay at Lucky's absence upon her return to herself in order to avoid creating an atmosphere which might have proved off-putting to Phil. Sophie's first night back in *Paradise* had not been a comfortable one. In addition to the uneasy feeling created by the threatening note she had had to deal with the onset of 'that time of the month'. She had decided against staying the night at the Spencers' home, feeling that if she allowed herself that luxury it would be detrimental to her efforts to settle back in at home. Also she didn't trust herself to accompany William to the airport; she felt that the risk that she would break down and beg him not to go was greater than ever.

She turned and looked at him, trying to think where to begin. There were so many things she wanted to say to him, and so little time left in which to say them. Ten minutes: ten pathetic little minutes!

Imogen took Dudley by the arm and steered him in the direction of the house. 'We'll go and do the washing up,' she told Sophie emphatically as they passed. The understanding between the two women was now such that it was obvious to Sophie that Imogen was conscious of her predicament, and she did not feel the need to feign a protest.

In any case Sophie was still staring, transfixed at William, reluctantly acknowledging a disquieting realisation. On several occasions people had remarked on the resemblance between William and Timmy, but now she identified in her boyfriend's open mouth and sparkling eyes an expression of juvenile exuberance, which gave the similarity between uncle and nephew a newfound poignancy.

Words were still failing her. William, however, had finished contemplating exciting possibilities and was eager to speak:

'Hey, Sophie, did you hear what Toby was telling me?'

The absence of a response did not deter him from continuing:

'Well, a colleague of his has just come back from a holiday in space and he had a fantastic time! He said that the games you can play at the Moonville space resort are really something else! And did you know…'

'Stop it! Stop it!' Sophie broke in, seizing both ends of his open shirt collar and burying her head in the middle of his chest. After a moment she jerked her head back and began to administer delicate blows to his torso with her crumpled little hands, alternating left and right – blows which lacked the force to hurt him but which were sufficient to communicate her vexation. William had to clasp her wrists together in order to stop her.

'What's wrong?' he wanted to know, suddenly very perturbed, but Sophie's eruption of grief had overwhelmed her, rendering her incapable of a reply. The sound of Sophie's sobs had drawn Imogen back out to the porch, and William looked helplessly towards his mother.

Still unaware of Imogen's presence, Sophie suddenly found her voice:

'What's come over you? All you can think about is your bloody holiday! What about Anita? You've forgotten all about her! Anita's dead! My friend is dead! Murdered! And my dad might be next! Or it could be me, William! Has that even crossed your mind? These people are so full of hate they don't care who they hurt. How does that make you feel, William? I know how I feel. I'm angry. I'm afraid. But you're too busy thinking about the games you're going to be playing on the bloody moon! Until all this happened I used to think of you as someone who really cared. Now…' She paused for a moment, shook her head, and then looked him directly in the eyes. 'Now I'm not so sure.'

Imogen took a step forward, placed her hand on her son's shoulder and said simply: 'Go and help your father.' William hesitated for a few seconds and then consented. Putting her arm around Sophie, Imogen guided her indoors and sat her down on the sofa in the lounge. She dried her tears, fetched her a glass of martini and held her close, caring for her as if she were her own daughter.

The sound of the doorbell indicated that Phil had arrived. Dudley asked if he would mind waiting for a few minutes. 'Sure,' they heard him reply, and he went back out to the car.

When Imogen felt that Sophie was ready she led her to the kitchen door. Dudley had gone out the back to empty the dustbin. William, his own distress now visible, reached up and put his right hand on her cheek, gently raising her drooping head until their eyes met once again.

'I'll make it up to you when I get back, I promise.' He refrained from attempting a kiss. She smiled weakly; then, unable to bring herself to say goodbye, she turned and made her way to the front door without further ado.

'Take care,' William called after her.

Imogen saw her to the car. Phil had turned the vehicle round in readiness. Seeing them approach in the interior mirror, he got out and opened the rear passenger door. The two women exchanged a hug, and Sophie took her seat behind Phil.

'Thanks,' she managed, as Imogen bent down to take a final look at her before closing the door.

The reply took the form of a wink and a kindly smile. 'Call me soon,' she added.

Phil started the engine and they set off down the drive. Unaware of the situation which had just arisen and feeling that he should initiate a conversation he tried to catch a glimpse of Sophie in the mirror, but she was sitting too close to the door for him to see her.

'So,' he began uncertainly as he checked to the right and left at the bottom of the drive, 'did you have a good evening?'

Chapter 11

Sunshine was glaring in through the glass of the south-facing window of the bedroom; it was the extra warmth it generated which finally woke Sophie up that Wednesday morning. A glance at the small digital clock on her bedside table confirmed that it was only just appropriate to think of this time of day as morning. Remembering she had some preparation to complete for the lessons she was due to give later that afternoon she resolved to get moving. Donning a sky blue silk dressing gown she took a look out of the other window – the one which looked in the direction of Maplehurst. In the foreground stood the wing to the rear of the mansion where the indoor swimming pool was located. Adjacent to this room was another which in her mother's lifetime had been used for buffets, meetings and other gatherings. It was the room around which the fifty-seventh birthday party was to have taken place. It was partly due to the fact that it brought back painful memories, and partly because they had not found any suitable alternative use for it, that since that day it had been rarely visited for purposes other than cleaning.

Until yesterday. That Tuesday morning as Sophie lay in bed contemplating the events of the night before she had heard a delivery vehicle arriving – a large truck almost the same size as the ones they had used when they first moved into *Paradise*. She had watched as three deliverymen in green uniforms had unloaded various boxes, most of which were large and flat, whereas a few were more upright and crate-like. Phil helped while Lucky oversaw the operation. Through the windows she had observed the men working inside the room; gradually the floor became covered with what looked like a rather uneven green carpet.

By the time she had bathed and dressed the delivery vehicle had gone. Neither Lucky nor Phil had returned from the rear wing. Her curiosity to know what was happening did battle with her craving for her regular breakfast time bowl of cornflakes: the former emerged victorious. As she walked along the side of the indoor pool she heard a cheer coming towards her. Opening the door she peered round before entering, not quite knowing what to expect.

'I'll tell you what, it was as well there was plenty of backspin on that one, otherwise it would have ended up in the drink,' Lucky remarked excitedly to Phil, who was bending over something on the room's new surface, but who had noticed Sophie's arrival out of the corner of his eye. The direction of Phil's gaze alerted Lucky to his daughter's presence.

'Well, come on in then!' Lucky called to her. Sophie was beginning to make sense of what was happening. Lucky was standing on a mat in front of a semi-circular screen on which appeared the image of a small grass-covered island connected to the mainland by a jetty. A yellow flag could be seen towards the back of this area. The surface on which Phil was crouching mirrored this image; there was even a flag in the equivalent position.

Between them Lucky and Phil explained how the apparatus worked; a gadget behind the mat provided an astonishingly realistic simulation of a golf ball placed on a tee; Lucky swung a club to demonstrate how a ball would travel across the screen and land either on the island or in the water surrounding it. A shot on target would cause a spot of light to appear on the room's new green carpet, until one of them replaced it with a golf ball; the ball could then be putted into the hole in the normal way. Lucky and Phil agreed that the grass-like texture of the surface meant that it was just like the real thing in this respect. All in all it lived up to its billing as "the ultimate in golfing practice equipment".

Sophie was persuaded to have a go on the mat, but even with Phil's patient instruction, every shot fell into the water. 'It's just a matter of practice,' he assured her. 'You would get the hang of it if you persevered.' Lucky, who had disappeared into the house to fetch some coffee, returned and told Phil that he had phoned the golf course and booked a starting time of 11.30 a.m. Sophie's initial reaction was one of astonishment that they were not satisfied with simply using the new practice facilities. Then she realised that this would mean she would be alone in *Paradise* for the first time since her return, and an uncomfortable feeling came over her.

Phil checked his watch: 'I was going to teach you how to putt, but I know you wanted me to take you through the ins and outs of the security system. There won't be time for both now. Which would you prefer to do?'

Sophie's response was unequivocal, and so Phil led her to the room upstairs which had been chosen to house the hub of the system. He showed her how to select a particular area on the estate on which to focus. Sophie was surprised to discover that it was even possible to pick up sounds, although the only conversations audible to them at this time were those between the blue tits which inhabited the bushes which bordered most of the estate. Sophie was impressed by the way in which Phil had familiarised himself with the intricacies of the system in such a short space of time and she told him so. He reminded her of his previous assurance that she should feel quite safe there. She smiled and nodded. Somehow Phil inspired confidence in people, and already she was beginning to feel secure as long as he was around.

In fact her first experience of solitude had been uneventful. It had been helped by the fact that several pupils had arrived for lessons late in the afternoon, and that the golfers had returned before dark. Now as Sophie looked down on the scene of the previous day's unexpected arrival she could see that they were in there, practising again. At the breakfast table she received another surprise. A letter had been left on the table from the golf club acknowledging receipt of payment of an annual subscription. Knowing that her father had renewed his own membership some time ago she deduced that he must have paid for Phil to join the club. Although the sum involved was not substantial in comparison to her father's resources, it was unlike him to be so generous. There was no question he was enjoying having Phil around; indeed she was astonished at how well the pair were getting on.

When Lucky came into the room he had a broad grin on his face:

'I suppose there's no need to ask where you're going!' Sophie remarked.

'That's right!' Lucky replied. He took some scorecards from his pocket. 'Look at these!' he said proudly. Sophie flicked through them. 'I've knocked a shot off my best score twice in the last week. That's because I'm playing with someone who can actually give me a game for once.'

'So that's why you've paid for his membership?' she deduced.

'Yeah, I suppose it is really. You know, whoever wrote that daft note did me a big favour!'

'I'm glad you can see it that way! And I wish you were as generous to William. It's as much as you can do to buy him a birthday present!'

'Well, I can't help it. The thing is William's one of these academic types. His head's full of legal jargon, but what does he know about life, eh? Now Todd is a real man. Someone who wouldn't let you down in a crisis.'

'What do you mean?'

'Well, what did William do when he saw the gunman that evening, eh? Did he try to do anything about it? No, he went and hid behind a tree!'

'Dad, he was protecting me!'

'Well, he could have made sure you were hidden and then tried to stop them.'

'But the man had a gun! How could he have stopped them with just his bare hands?'

'He could have distracted them, or at least raised the alarm! But no, he waits until the coast is clear before he does anything!'

Lucky shook his head disgustedly. 'Take it from me, if it had been me or Todd, we would have done something.' He paused and waited in vain for a response. 'Think about it,' he added; then he turned to the intercom system and flicked the switch which enabled him to get through to the golf practice room. 'Come on Todd, let's go!' he called out.

Lucky looked for a moment in the direction of Sophie, who was still sitting in stunned silence. 'See you later,' he said simply. As he left the room the grin had returned to his face.

'I'm sorry, what did you say?' William asked, turning away from the window through which he had appeared to be looking for some minutes.

'I said, this time tomorrow we will have landed at Moonville.'

William nodded, but made no attempt to develop the conversation.

'Is something wrong?' Jack wanted to know.

'No, I was just thinking.' There was a pause, during which Jack looked curiously at William. Then he spoke again:

'I don't want to appear nosy, but if you want to talk about it, let me know.'

'Okay,' William nodded; then he smiled briefly. 'Thanks,' he added.

He looked away again in the direction of the unending darkness. The absence of visible distractions had served to emphasise his mood. Sophie's outburst had taken the wind right out of his sails. As he had boarded the plane at Gatwick he had thought for the first time that he might come to regret having taken this trip. As he walked down the gangway towards the waiting stewardess he had stopped momentarily, teasing himself with the possibility of a last minute change of mind. As he stood there and hesitated someone had knocked into him from behind and this had set him in motion again. Sophie would have said it was a reminder that he had an appointment with destiny to keep. It was so ironic, he reflected as he boarded the plane; here was an opportunity few people in the course of history had ever had, and it had come to him for nothing on account of the fact that he had parents who were both rich and generous, and at the last minute something had happened which might prevent him from enjoying the experience.

During the flight Jack Macgregor had tapped him on the shoulder and introduced himself. It transpired that he had spotted William carrying the special suitcase which the space travel company supplied as part of the package. Old enough to be William's grandfather, Jack explained that he had been suddenly widowed earlier in the year and had decided to fulfil a longstanding ambition in an attempt to get his life back on a positive footing. William had been relieved to discover that he was not going to be the only English passenger on the spaceship, and had initially derived some comfort from Jack's constant desire to converse, especially in view of the fact that he was very knowledgeable about what lay in store for them, but increasingly he had come to wish for some solitude and for the chance to contemplate.

Not that this activity was either pleasant or productive. As William stared out of the window of the spaceship, he was reliving the moment when he had first spotted the attacker approaching the house. He asked himself, not for the first time, whether there was more he could have done. He wondered how long had elapsed between the first sight of the man carrying the gun and the explosion. Ten seconds? Twenty at most. Perhaps just enough time to get to the man. But then what could he have expected to achieve? The most likely outcome would have been that he would have simply added his own name to the list of victims.

Then again, what if he had not waited so long to come out from his hiding place? Might he have been able to save Melissa? He recalled the glimpse he had caught of the fleeing attacker. What if he had thought to set off in pursuit? Might he have been able to trail him to the getaway vehicle and take the registration number, or even take action himself. As he pictured the moment in his mind's eye something struck him.

Something he had not recollected before, perhaps because at first he had struggled to suppress the memory in order to put the whole thing behind him. Both the gunman he saw approaching the house and the man he saw running away were tall and stocky with masks and grey hair – but William was sure that as the attacker made his getaway he was not carrying a gun. He couldn't remember whether the detective who had interviewed him had checked this point. He felt certain that if the police had found a gun at the scene he would have heard about this. In any case, he reasoned, it was unlikely that the attacker would have left it behind. If he was right, this could only mean one thing: that the similarity was a coincidence and there was more than one attacker. He resolved to make this known to the police on his return. Unless of course they had already caught the culprits. William imagined Sophie feeling scared and unhappy in *Paradise* and prayed that they had indeed been apprehended.

An old white Mini Metro parked unevenly in a space in a car park in Horsham town centre. Its two occupants got out and walked along the road to the police station. The stern faced middle-aged woman opened the door and ushered her son through it and on into the reception. The young man had a dishevelled look and a spotty countenance, from which one might have deduced wrongly that he was still in his teens. At the counter the sergeant returned and apologetically informed an old lady that her missing ring had not been handed in; she thanked him and turned to go.

The sergeant wanted to know how he could help the new arrivals, causing the woman to look shamefully at the young man. The prompt was ignored, and it fell to the woman to answer.

'My son,' she began gravely, pointing an accusing finger at him, 'has something to confess.'

Chapter 12

'I know it's a very beautiful time of year, it's just that I hate the way the nights are drawing in. I really only like summer,' Sophie told Phil, who nodded in agreement.

'How long do you spend in the gym?' Sophie asked.

'About an hour and a half.' He paused and thought for a moment. 'I don't have to stay there that long if you've had enough before then.'

'No, that's fine. I'll walk around the grounds, and then have a swim. Thanks anyway.'

As Sophie smiled across at Phil she realised that she had got into the front of his car without hesitation. She had become accustomed to his presence, and her concern that he wouldn't stay with them had disappeared. In fact, Phil had settled into a routine on which he appeared to be thriving. He would get up early and visit the gym, returning in time for lunch; then he would accompany her father to the golf course, usually followed by a drink in the bar, before returning for the evening meal which she would cook for them. Afterwards, Phil would read, while Sophie played the piano or watched the television with her father before going to bed, then Phil would go for a lengthy swim in the indoor pool. He seemed to have an insatiable appetite for fitness enhancing activities, and little time for socialising. A couple of male friends had come to visit in the evenings, but there was no evidence of a girlfriend. He appeared quite content living a bachelor's existence. Sophie suddenly found herself voicing her thoughts aloud:

'Phil,' she began, 'are you happy?'

He smiled warmly, both surprised and touched at her inquiry.

'Yes, I suppose I am really. Thanks for asking.'

He was about to return the question, when Sophie came up with another:

'What do you think about what Dad's doing? I mean, I assume he's told you about this clinic he's attending which is giving him this life-extending substance.'

‘Oh yes, I know all about it.’

‘So what do you think?’

‘Oh, I think it’s great.’ He smiled across at her. ‘If I had the money, I would be joining him like a shot.’

An idea struck Sophie, and she opened her mouth to give voice to it, but stopped herself in the nick of time. She would have to speak to her father first. Instead, she merely expressed her surprise at their arrival at the gym.

Jack reached out and placed his hand on William’s arm. ‘Don’t you think you would feel better if you talked about it?’ he asked softly.

‘You’re right,’ William replied, without turning to face the older man. He was fighting to hold back the tears, and he was concerned that the slightest eye contact would open the taps and cause a flood.

There was a pause while William calmed himself in preparation for his explanation. Jack waited patiently, then listened intently to the whole tale: Lucky’s involvement with the clinic, the night at the Burkin’s, Sophie’s subsequent malaise, and the disastrous last evening at home. Jack himself was obviously moved by William’s recollections of these events, to the extent that his eyes began to water. Noticing this, William began to loosen his fragile grasp on his emotions, until eventually both men were weeping openly. Other passengers noticed, and gave them curious looks, but they were too involved in their heart-to-heart discussions to realise, let alone feel embarrassment.

‘Do you think I’ve lost her?’ William asked finally.

Jack thought for a moment before replying.

‘It’s not easy to say for sure, especially as I don’t even know her, except for what you’ve told me. You haven’t done anything unforgivable. It’s mainly just unfortunate timing. It’s a shame it’s such a long trip. Still, we’re just past halfway. Oh, what a pity you haven’t been able to enjoy it.’ He pondered a moment, then went on:

'The most important thing is to make sure she knows how much you care. What have you got lined up when you get back?'

'I'll be starting my new job within about ten days.'

'See if you can postpone it. Then just spend the whole of the rest of the time with her. Do things she likes doing, take her mind off what's happened. Make her feel really special.'

William nodded.

'In the meantime, keep sending her messages.'

'What do you mean?'

Jack looked puzzled:

'You mean you don't know? There's a system for sending messages to earth, for redistribution via e-mail to the person concerned.'

'There is?'

'Yes. Crumbs, William, you really have been living in a world of your own, haven't you?'

'Well, where is it? What do I have to do?'

Jack reached under his seat and pulled out a folder. He opened it and passed a notepad to William. 'Just write your message clearly on one of these special forms. Take it to the last room on the right, and put it through the processor. The whole thing is done automatically from there. So you can put whatever you like. It doesn't matter how personal.'

William's look betrayed mixed feelings. On the one hand, he was relieved that there was at least a chance of getting through to Sophie. On the other, he was exasperated that the opportunity had been there all along, if only he had known.

'I take it she has got a computer,' Jack asked.

'Yes, although she doesn't switch it on very often. Her dad does, though, so hopefully he'll pass it on.'

'Good,' Jack asserted.

William took out a pen and began to think what to write. He decided he would show the message to Jack before sending it, in the hope of benefiting further from his wisdom.

A question sprang to mind:

'Do you mind if I ask how long you were married?'

Jack smiled benignly.

'Fifty-five years,' he replied.

William understood where the wisdom had come from.

'And do you know what my wife's name was?' Jack went on.

'Let me guess,' said William.

'Sophie!' The two men spoke in unison. Then they laughed a little, looked warmly at each other, took out their hankies and wiped the moisture from their faces.

Chapter 13

It had seemed an ordinary morning to Phil as he returned to *Paradise*. On this occasion Sophie had not accompanied him to the gym, saying she had something to discuss with her father. As he stopped his car near the row of seven garages he was pondering the consequences of the news bulletin he had just heard on the radio. When Sophie opened the front door and hurried down the steps with a broad smile on her face he assumed she had heard too. Her opening remarks, however, suggested otherwise:

'Will you take me down to the village?' she asked, inclining her head slightly, still smiling.

'Sure.'

'Good, because I have something to tell you.'

She closed the passenger door. Phil looked at her inquisitively as he set off down the drive.

'You know the other day we were talking about the clinic, and you said you would jump at the chance to have treatment there if you had the money.'

'Yes.' Phil looked puzzled.

'Well, my dad has been trying for some time to get me to be treated there. I think I've finally persuaded him it's not for me. Anyway, I put it to him that he could use the money he set aside to pay for you to go there.'

Phil's expression suggested he doubted what he was hearing. Sophie realised an explanation was required.

'Phil, I don't know how well you've been able to get to know my dad over the past few weeks, but I'm sure he would be the first to admit, he's a very selfish person. So don't think of this as a particularly generous gesture on his part. He can easily afford it and it happens to suit him nicely. You see, the idea of arranging protection for him was mine – in fact I insisted on it. As far as he's concerned you are more of a companion. The truth is he hates being alone, and since you are both so keen on golf you keep him amused and occupied.

So you shouldn't feel indebted to him, and you certainly shouldn't hesitate to accept. Just think of it as a fortunate coincidence of needs.'

Phil was still giving her the same incredulous look.

'So what do you say? Will you accept?' Sophie asked eagerly.

Phil shrugged his shoulders, thought for a moment, then nodded: 'Well, I suppose so. If you're sure.'

'Oh great! I'm so pleased. Now can we stop at the corner shop here?'

Phil obliged. Sophie smiled at him and continued:

'Come on in. I'm going to buy some wine to have with this evening's meal, by way of celebration. You can help me choose.'

Inside the corner shop they perused the selection of Australian Chardonnay, which Sophie had discovered was Phil's favourite. As they queued to pay she remembered something else she had meant to say.

'Oh yes, and I checked with Dad that it won't make any difference if they catch the killers. He will still keep you on and carry on paying for the treatment.'

This last comment reminded Phil of what had been concerning him as he had been about to park the car.

'That's good to know,' he observed, 'especially after what I've just heard on the radio.'

Sophie felt a twinge of excitement.

'What was that?' she demanded to know.

'The police have arrested a man in connection with the murders.'

Sophie almost jumped for joy and flung her arms around Phil. Only the bodyguard's formidable reactions prevented the bottle of wine from being knocked from his hand.

As William slowly floated back to his usual seat Jack looked up at him hopefully. The response took the form of a doleful shake of the head.

'That passenger who had a fit of space rage the other day vandalised the system. They doubt whether they will be able to get it working again before we get back.' William's frustration was etched on his face.

'Never mind, in a week's time we'll be back on earth,' Jack replied, but his attempt to give reassurance was unsuccessful.

'If only I knew all was well. Right now I would settle for knowing I would be given a chance to patch things up when I get back.' He looked solemnly at the older man, whose wrinkled features exhibited real concern. 'Something's wrong. I don't know what it is, or how I know, but it is.'

Jack wanted to disagree, but found himself unable to. So he just patted William's wrist a couple of times and gave him a sympathetic smile.

William held the message in both hands and stared down at it. He knew it by heart now, having re-read it so many times since he had first been informed that the system had crashed some days earlier:

'Dear Sophie, I am on the way back to earth now. The journey has had its moments. The launch was fantastic, as was walking in space. I have been to Moonville and written my name in the moon dust. There is nothing to disturb it, so it will stay there forever.

But I can't honestly say I am enjoying myself. I can't stop thinking about you. If I took you for granted, or if I didn't realise how you were feeling, then I'm really sorry. I can't wait to be back at home with you. I miss you terribly and love you so. William.'

All at once the sight of the unsent note became too much to bear. William's right hand became a clenched fist and the sheet of paper was crumpled into a ball in the middle of it. Then he tossed it upwards, whereupon it began to drift in the weightless atmosphere within the spacecraft, a little floating capsule of misery for all to behold.

Chapter 14

Sophie looked across at the digital alarm clock on top of her bedside table, just in time for the moment when 10: 59 p.m. turned to 11:00 p.m. Normally she would go straight off to sleep, but tonight she was tossing and turning. As well as the excitement of knowing that an arrest had been made, she was feeling the heat. Or rather she was aware of the warmth which was coming from within; a hot flush which she hadn't felt for some time had come over her. And she was aware of the moment which had been responsible for rekindling it…

She got up and crossed to the window, and took a look out at the moonlit sky. William was out there somewhere, she reflected, in a vessel too small to be visible to her. She felt guilty that she had not been thinking of him more often. Life in *Paradise* had been so much more pleasurable since Phil had arrived, and she was forced to admit that she had not missed William in the way she had expected to. Her gaze fell on the light which was pouring through the windows of the swimming pool. Usually Phil would draw the blinds across, but for some reason tonight he hadn't done so. Sophie caught sight of his head bobbing up and down as he approached the far end of the pool. He was cutting through the water with impressive ease. Just as he made the turn she noticed something about his long, muscular frame that took her by surprise. She squinted, checking that her vision wasn't deceiving her, or whether perhaps he was wearing pale swimming trunks. She watched for at least a minute, but was still uncertain. Was he really swimming completely naked? She could feel her heartbeat quickening, and felt a pang of guilt, as though she were being disloyal. She tore herself away from the window and returned to her bed, endeavouring to convince herself that it was just curiosity. But now as she lay on her side she knew there was no question of sleep. There were tingling sensations, little quivers of excitement, a fluttering of butterflies in the stomach. She tried lying completely still, hoping it would pass, but the craving continued. Feeling hotter still now, she crossed the room to the chest of drawers and looked for something lighter to wear. She picked out a black chiffon nightie, one that William had bought for her. It was a little too large for her, but she had not wanted to take it back in case he was upset. She tried to focus on William, but could not picture his face. Turning, she pulled the gown she had been wearing up over her head and let it fall to the floor.

Sophie could see that the light was still on in the pool. She edged nearer to the window; modesty restrained her from getting too close. Sophie looked down at the slick figure chopping through the water, faster still now that he had switched to front crawl. She still couldn't quite tell... A thought crossed her mind and her heart missed a beat. Had Phil left the blinds open deliberately in the hope she would see him and be compelled to observe this exhibition of extreme agility and virility? After all, he must have worked out that he would be visible to her from the bedroom window. Had he felt the same rush of excitement she had when she had hugged him that morning? She moved right up to the window now, throwing caution to the wind. After all there was no way anyone else would see her. She watched for some minutes, still breathing quickly, her unclad body all tingly, looking – indeed hoping – to see him glance in her direction.

Eventually he paused at the end of a length, taking a momentary breather before changing stroke. There! He looked towards her. She felt sure of it. Remembering her nudity she turned away. Her pulse was racing now. But still there was an uncomfortable feeling of guilt. If it weren't for William she would go down there straight away. But fidelity reached out and restrained her. Sophie put on the black nightie and sat on the bed. She tried again to visualise William, thinking back to the moment when he had pushed her up against the tree and protected her from harm – his moment of heroism – or was it cowardice as Lucky would have it? Instead of seeing William her mind's eye caught a glimpse of Anita. She remembered something her friend had said to her once: 'You know, you must be the only person I know who has only ever had one boyfriend!' It had seemed insignificant to her before, but now the desire to find out what it would be like to be with someone else – particularly someone as manly as Phil – was overwhelming. Perhaps William's absence was meant to be, she thought suddenly. The events which had led up to this moment all seemed to point in the same direction. There was only one thing to do. She had to find out. She reasoned that if she went down to the pool she was in no way doing anything to which she was committed. If she realised she was mistaken, she would have the opportunity to return to her room as though nothing had happened. If she did not go she would never know. It all made sense now. She had to…had to…go.

As she tiptoed barefoot towards the door to the swimming pool, she found herself praying, 'God, if I'm wrong, stop me!'

She turned the handle nervously and pushed. Phil was about half way along the pool, heading away from her. She could see clearly enough from this distance. There was Phil's bare bottom, wriggling enticingly as he swam. She had been right all along about that.

Sophie approached the pool and stood on the edge, positioning herself exactly where Phil would return to as he swam back. On reaching the far end of the pool, Phil paused again. Somehow he had sensed her arrival. Goodness knows how, she had been so quiet. He turned to face her. The light from the wall behind shone through the black nightie so that the outline of her slender body was clearly visible. As he looked towards her she saw him flash her the same smile as on the first day they had met.

Immediately he began to swim towards her. Was it her imagination, she thought, or was he swimming even faster than usual? She wondered what she should do. Should she take off the nightgown and jump in to the pool, or should she just wait for him? A third possibility sprang to mind. Sophie sat down on the edge, dropped her legs in the water, and began to paddle, slowly, rhythmically, invitingly. She leaned backwards, allowed her head to fall back so that her hair was dangling, closed her eyes and waited to be pulled into the water.

Sophie's excitement was almost feverish now. She knew he was close. Any moment now she would feel his strong fingers grabbing hold of her legs. The splashing sounds got louder…and louder…and still louder…until finally they stopped. For a few seconds there was nothing. Sophie opened her eyes and brought her head up to see where exactly he was. He had stopped nearby, his hands clutching the edge of the pool. He looked up at her and smiled again, then said simply: 'Hi.' Then he took a deep breath, turned round onto his front and began to swim away.

Chapter 15

Sophie deliberately waited until after Phil had gone to the gym before she came down for breakfast the following morning. His failure to respond to her in the way she had expected had left her feeling very disconsolate. She was confused as to whether he had even realised what she was intimating. In fact she rather hoped he hadn't, as this would lessen the embarrassment which she was sure to feel in his presence from now on. She concluded that even if he had not realised, it was clear that he wasn't attracted to her and she felt humiliated. She found to her surprise that the pain was actually physical. For some reason she was conscious of an aching sensation in the upper arms. Sophie was unused to rejection. A number of admirers had shown interest in her in recent years, but she had remained faithful to William. Now she felt guilty about her attempted infidelity. She would have to tell him at some point if they were going to get back together on his return. She remembered how he had not woken up when she had visited his room on the last night she had spent at his parents' house, and wondered whether he too had lost interest in her. Perhaps the effects of the trauma she had been through in recent weeks had made her somehow less attractive.

She had slept little that night. The feelings of arousal which had so overwhelmed her had subsided once she had sobbed her way back to her bed. Many times during the night she had struggled in vain to picture her mother, or even to hear her voice. It seemed that even Sophie's normally vivid imagination had deserted her. As she looked in the mirror that morning the face she saw had a ghost-like appearance. There was a rather strained, crestfallen look about her. The sparkle in her eyes had turned to sadness. She wondered whether this was the result of the previous night's rejection, or could it rather be the cause of it?

On her way to breakfast she had taken a detour to the front door to retrieve the papers. She glanced at the date of *The*

Independent. It was Wednesday 20th October. It was exactly one week before William was due back. At least she had some time to prepare her explanation. She hurried to the breakfast table, eager to begin perusing the newspaper, confident that it would contain further details of the previous day's announcement. Surely this would at least go some way towards cheering her up.

The article was on the front page: 'Sussex massacre – man arrested'. She was about to read on when the phone rang. She went to answer it but Lucky, who was coming down the stairs, beat her to it.

'Yes,' he began. 'Speaking…hello inspector.' Sophie's ears pricked up. There was a long pause while Lucky listened to the policeman's explanation for making the call. Sophie came and stood in front of her father, looking for clues in his facial expressions. Lucky was a man who gave little away, except when he was angry, and there was no flush in his cheeks. 'Are you sure?' he asked the inspector. There was another long pause. Sophie waited with mounting anxiety. She caught her father's eyes for a moment; then he turned away in order to concentrate on what he was being told. 'I hope you are going to press charges, anyway,' she heard him say; 'I see,' he added shortly afterwards. At last the conversation drew to a close; 'Okay, I'll keep my eyes open. Right. Thanks. Bye.'

'Well?' Sophie demanded.

Infuriatingly, Lucky prolonged her suspense still further by pausing for thought, before replying:

'The man who came into the station yesterday admitted to sending the death threat notes, including mine.'

'Good!'

'Yes, but he's not the murderer. It's as I thought. He's one of those batty protesters. Some sad kid with nothing better to do with his life. He owned up to sending about ten notes in all. They know it can't be him because the evening you were at the Burkins he was at one of their meetings. He was caught on video, sitting in the front row. He was definitely there all evening.'

Sophie sighed: 'So the killers are still free.'

'Yeah! But at least we know that the death threat was a hoax. So there's no reason to think they are targeting me.'

Sophie nodded her head. She agreed with the conclusion, but for some reason she derived little solace from it.

As the Ultramobile came to a halt in the designated spot and opened its doors to them Sophie realised that this was the first time she had travelled in the sports car since that fateful day in August when she had gone with her father to the clinic. This time she sat in the back, allowing Phil to sit in the front passenger seat. She had noticed that the atmosphere between Phil and Lucky seemed a little strained over the past few days, and had it in mind to find out what was wrong. The absence of the usual banter between them on the journey to the pub served to confirm her suspicions.

Inside the White Horse they settled into a corner to the rear of the bar. Phil stayed with them for a drink, but when they began looking at the food menu he excused himself, saying that he wanted to visit a friend who lived almost opposite. Sophie noticed that Lucky raised his eyebrows somewhat suspiciously on hearing this.

'I wonder what sort of "friend" he's going to see,' Lucky commented as he watched through the window of the pub while Phil waited to cross the road.

Now Sophie was even more bemused.

'What do you mean?'

Lucky turned and looked directly at her.

'You don't know what I'm getting at?'

'No, I have no idea.'

'Haven't you wondered why you never hear him talk about girlfriends? Or why he never has any women visiting him?'

'Well, yes I had wondered.'

'Hmm! Well, the reason is he's…you know…one of them.'

Sophie's jaw dropped.

'You mean he's…?'

Lucky nodded solemnly: 'Gay.'

Suddenly it all fell into place: the absence of women in his life, his lack of a response to her in the pool, her father's newfound aloofness to him on account of his homophobia.

'How do you know?' she asked.

'He told me so. One of the barmaids at the golf club was very cut up the other day because he had turned her down, so I asked him why.'

As they ate their meals Sophie considered the revelation. She found that it lifted the burden of the sense of rejection she had been feeling, now that she knew it was nothing personal. As the evening progressed, and her favourite martini soothed her, she started to feel quite light-hearted. For the first time in a couple of months she began to contemplate the possibility of a return to normal. The memory of her ordeal was receding, the death threat against her father had turned out to be a hoax, and William was due back the following day. Sophie told Lucky she wanted to meet him from the airport in the evening, and her father agreed to ask Phil to take her. She had previously established that Lucky intended to retain Phil's services despite the recent arrest, but now she felt moved to ask again. He replied in the affirmative. Presumably Phil's recent admission was not sufficient to make him want to dismiss his golfing companion.

As she took the last sip from her martini glass it occurred to her to check whether Lucky was still intending to pay for Phil to attend the clinic. Before she had the chance to speak, however, she caught sight of Phil walking briskly towards their table. He looked towards her as he approached. The concern on his face made her suddenly very uneasy. He did not stop to acknowledge them before speaking:

'When does William get back?'

'Tomorrow evening. Why?'

'Is that when his plane touches down, or when his spacecraft returns to earth?'

'That's when his plane arrives. His spacecraft is due in this evening. Why? What's the matter?'

The look on Phil's face was graver now.

'Terrorists have shot down a spacecraft as it came into land today.'

Sophie screamed: 'No, no, oh please, God, no!' In her anguish she clamped both hands to her face.

Other diners in the pub looked round to see what was going on.

'There's a phone number here for people concerned about relatives,' added Phil.

He held out a piece of paper. Sophie grabbed it, as a drowning man clutches at a straw. Her hands were trembling so much that she could hardly hold it still enough to read the number.

'Has anyone got a phone?' she managed to ask.

Lucky shook his head: 'I haven't got mine with me.'

'Here,' said a woman from the adjacent table, 'use mine.'

She held it out towards Sophie, who tried to take it from her, but her quivering hands were unable to keep hold of it, and it fell under the table. Sophie dived down after it, disappearing altogether as she rummaged around. Lucky peered beneath the table, but couldn't see it. Phil spotted it under the chair and abruptly retrieved it. Sophie knocked her head on the table as she resurfaced, but in her panic she failed even to notice the pain.

Phil took the piece of paper back from Sophie. 'I'll dial the number,' he said calmly. Sophie waited, panting tearfully, while Phil pressed the required keys on the phone. He checked that it was ringing, before passing it to her. Her wrist was shaking so much that she had difficulty keeping the phone steady enough to enable her to hear whether the call had been answered. The woman who had lent Sophie the phone reached out, took her other hand, and squeezed it. All eyes were fixed on Sophie now. The atmosphere became hushed, to the extent that a young couple who had just come into the bar immediately sensed that something was wrong and joined the transfixed onlookers.

'Come on, come on!' Sophie cried out, willing the call to be answered. Sophie's blurred gaze fell on the woman clutching her hand. Finally a voice came on the other end of the line. There was silence all around as Sophie answered the questions in a wavering voice:

'Spencer.' There was a pause.

'William… I'm his girlfriend.'

There followed another pause. It lasted a few seconds, but it seemed to last forever. Then Sophie fell to her knees, tottered for a moment, and finally collapsed face downwards onto the floor, sobbing uncontrollably.

It was Phil who reached down and helped her up, managing to get her back onto the seat in an upright position. Finally she was able to gain control of the tears. And then, against everyone's expectations, she let out an enormous sigh of relief.

Chapter 16

The first of the special suitcases provided by the space travel company came along the conveyor belt. They checked it and found that it belonged to Jack. A minute or so later the other suitcase appeared. William retrieved it and turned nervously to the older man.

'Well, now's the moment of truth.'

Jack nodded.

'If she's here you'll know she still cares. If she isn't, it's not necessarily the end of the world.'

'Whatever happens, I'll write and let you know how things turn out. Thanks for everything, Jack.'

They made their way towards the exit. The volume of passengers converging on the gateway with their luggage meant that progress was slow. William's heart was beginning to pound. As the two men came through into the arrivals lounge, William began to scan the faces of those waiting for loved ones. He caught a glimpse of his father, whose height enabled him to see over the heads of those standing in front. As William picked his way through the crowd he caught sight of his mother, standing next to his father. But there was no sign of Sophie. William's parents reached out to their son, hugged him and kissed him.

'Thank God you're safe,' said Imogen. 'It was a nasty shock, hearing about the other spacecraft. Fortunately we knew yours had already touched down.'

'Thank goodness for that. I wondered if you might have thought it was mine.'

William introduced Jack, who had been patiently waiting behind him. Then he sought confirmation of what he had feared:

'I don't suppose Sophie's here?'

'We tried to ring her last night to see whether she was coming, but she was out,' Dudley explained.

William looked crestfallen.

'I spoke to her several times while you were away. She's all right,' Imogen assured him in an attempt to cheer him up.

'It's over,' William muttered, turning towards his mother. As he did so, he became aware of someone running towards him, calling his name. Before he had had the chance to take in what was happening, Sophie was upon him, her arms locked around him, showering him with kisses.

It was cold enough that Thursday morning for Sophie to take out her winter coat for the first time. The air in St. Leonard's forest was crisp and still, and as she and William walked hand in hand along a path which was yet to consume sufficient rainwater to have become muddy, there were few sounds in the air to compete with William's chatter.

Perhaps it was the relief that she had been there to welcome him, or perhaps it was the excitement of the trip, Sophie could not tell for sure, but he had hardly stopped talking. She was left in no doubt about how much he had been thinking about her while he was away. The experience had given him a greater sense of perspective, he told her. Beforehand he hadn't quite finished growing up; now he would make sure he had his priorities right. Remembering Jack's advice, William had contacted his employers first thing that morning and arranged for his starting date to be delayed so that they could spend some quality time together. He pledged that once he had begun his career he would work hard in order ensure a better future for them both.

The last remark had really taken Sophie by surprise. It was so unlike William to make such plans, she reflected. And it was clear that he envisaged spending his future with her. She knew he was aware that this had always been her desire. And now, ironically, just as he was starting to think ahead, just as he was beginning to act in a way which could bring their relationship to fruition, she was going to have to make a confession which might put an end to everything.

She had hoped to persuade herself that there was no need to say anything. After all nothing had happened. She had just made a mistake; that was all. But she had realised that if she didn't tell him there would always be an unspoken truth lurking in her mind, something she had not dared to tell him, something which he ought to know about her and did not know – an indiscretion for which he should have been granted the chance to decide whether he could forgive her, and had not been.

And so she had resolved to tell him. But was now the right time, or would it be better to have some happy times first?

As they arrived back at the car, she could see that he had noticed her unease.

'What's the matter?' he asked softly.

Sophie felt that if she explained straight away it would make for a very fraught ride back to *Paradise*.

'I'll tell you when we get home.'

'Why not tell me now?'

'No, William, please take me home first.'

'Okay, if you insist.' As he opened the passenger door of his father's MG and let her take her seat he suddenly looked very concerned.

On the short journey back from the forest the atmosphere was heavy with tension. William resisted the temptation to speed. He found himself glancing across at Sophie whenever he had the chance and recalled the journey to the Burkins', a reminder which fuelled his alarm.

Because of the alterations to the security system, they had to wait at the gates for Lucky to let them in. William could see the apprehension in Sophie's eyes now. At last he brought the sports car to a standstill near the fountain in the centre of the forecourt.

A few minutes later the vehicle was in motion again. Sophie watched anxiously as it headed steadily for the gates, which closed behind it as it turned onto the road. William concentrated on driving safely, trying to ignore the lump which had formed in his throat, and the confusion which he was going to have to resolve in his mind if their relationship was to continue. Little snippets of Sophie's revelation came back to him as he drove slowly home: '…there's something I must tell you…nothing actually happened…I just got everything muddled up in my head that night…it was just physical attraction…if it had not been for the way things were between us before you left…maybe we both still had some growing up to do… I realise now how much I love you…I'll try again if you will…' Amidst the turmoil he tried to focus on the positive words with which she had concluded. She would try again if he would. Despite his pain he couldn't help remarking on the irony: instead of having to seek her forgiveness for his lack of sensitivity, it was now a question of whether he could come to terms with what she had told him. He had been dealt a bitter blow, completely out of the blue. His reaction had been more one of shock than anger. All he could do now was go away and think about it, and see whether time would enable the wounds to heal.

Chapter 17

Looking across at the dashboard from the rear seat of the Ultramobile Sophie noticed with dismay the six digits relating to the date: 02:11:09. She always found November a gloomy month. December at least boasted the cheer and brightness associated with Christmas. In January and February the dreariness returned. The atmosphere in *Paradise* over the weekend had been sombre. There had been no word as yet from William, and she had with great difficulty kept to her resolve not to contact him first. She wanted to give him the chance to consider the situation without any interference from her.

The previous evening, a Monday, she had taken the opportunity to ask Phil's opinion of William's conduct on the evening of the massacre. She had put herself through the ordeal of reliving the experience in detail in order to be sure of conveying an accurate impression of his reactions. Phil's response was unequivocal. Even with appropriate training, it would have been highly dangerous to tackle an armed man; without such instruction it would have been very foolish. To attempt to intervene would have needlessly endangered his life and perhaps hers too. Sophie mentioned her father's opinion. Phil dismissed it with a smile, saying it was impossible to know how one would act in such a situation until the time arose.

Later, while Phil had gone for his nightly swim, Sophie reminded her father that they were due to attend the Walton Foundation the following morning. Lucky revealed that he regretted agreeing to pay for Phil to attend the clinic and was intending to tell him that he had had second thoughts. Sophie had expressed her disgust that he could even consider doing this. The fact that she resorted to threatening to leave home if he did so had the desired effect. Hence they had kept the appointment at the clinic, and Phil had undergone the first instalment of the treatment, while Lucky had received the 'top up' to which Dr Braithwaite had alluded on their previous visit.

The contrast between that sweltering day in August and the iciness of this present one could hardly have been greater. Before returning home, they had visited the same pub in which Sophie had learned of Dr Walsingham's murder. Perhaps it was this unwelcome reminder, coupled with the fact that Lucky had ignored her pleas and had several drinks before driving back to *Paradise*, which was making her feel so uncomfortable now. It was nearly five o'clock and darkness was beginning to fall.

It must have been her mounting anxiety which caused Sophie to glance out of the rear window of the Ultramobile. At first, she thought nothing of what she saw. Then, abruptly, she looked round again, trying to get a closer look at the vehicle behind – a white Vulcan with a black roof. Was it her imagination, or had it fallen back a little since she first looked round?

'That car behind us,' she began, causing Phil to look round from the front passenger seat, 'I think it's following us.'

'Oh, Sophie, you and your bloody imagination!' Lucky scoffed.

Phil knew better than to dismiss such assertions without investigation.

'What makes you think that?' he asked.

'There was one just like it behind us as we pulled into the pub car park.'

'Are you sure?'

'Yes.'

'Did you notice that?' Phil asked Lucky.

'No,' he replied immediately. 'But then I don't look in the mirror much,' he added, grinning.

Phil was keeping a keen eye on the car behind now. Sophie was dividing her attention between watching the vehicle and observing Phil's surveillance of it. The Vulcan had definitely dropped even further behind them now. They were coming up to a large roundabout.

'Look, if it makes you happy, I'll just put my foot down and we'll lose them,' Lucky suggested. The look on his face remained dismissive.

'No don't do that, go round this roundabout again and see whether they follow,' Phil asserted.

'Hey, hold on a minute, I'm driving this car,' Lucky resisted.

'Just do it, Dad!' Sophie snapped.

Lucky consented with a shrug of the shoulders. Missing out the right turn which he would normally have taken he completed a full circuit of the roundabout. The Vulcan followed them as far as their intended exit and disappeared along the road they would have gone down. Sophie saw enough of the driver to see that he had grey hair.

'So now what?' Lucky asked Phil.

'Let's take another way back.'

'Oh, you're joking. It'll take ages if we go the other way.'

'Better safe than sorry,' Phil concluded.

Ignoring the exit required for the alternative route, Lucky carried on round the roundabout until they again reached their intended turning. He pulled the Ultramobile over to the side of the road, stopping just short of the exit.

'I'm going to get giddy if we go round again!' he remarked.

The road was brightly lit and they could see quite a long way down it. Sophie could tell that her father was determined to go home the way he had planned.

'Dad, don't go down that road,' she implored him. 'They could be waiting for us down there.'

'Look,' Lucky began, 'the car's gone. There's no sign of it.'

'Even so…' Phil began.

'Listen, I want to get home because there's something I want to watch on the television. There's no reason to think we were being followed, and even if we were, this vehicle's built like a tank. So what are we waiting for?'

Phil shook his head in exasperation: 'Why do you have to place yourself in danger unnecessarily?'

'Not to mention us!' Sophie chimed in.

'Look, I'm not going to be intimidated! I'm going home the normal way. Anyone who hasn't got the bottle doesn't have to come with me. There's a bus stop just round the corner.' Lucky glared at Phil and then over his shoulder at Sophie. Their response was one of stunned silence.

Lucky could wait no longer: he set the Ultramobile in motion and rounded the corner into the road which had been the subject of the dispute. They travelled on in silence. Phil found himself scrutinising the oncoming vehicles, as well as keeping an eye on the junctions they passed. He glanced to the rear occasionally, but nothing came from behind them. Few vehicles would have been able to catch the Ultramobile, especially as Lucky was now driving even faster than usual, seemingly intent on making up for lost time. Phil was gradually forming the conclusion that Sophie's suspicions were unfounded.

Soon the road narrowed and ceased to be well lit. It was just gone five o'clock and the gathering gloom aggravated Sophie's apprehension. Still nobody spoke. Raindrops began to appear on the windows, impeding Sophie's efforts to remain vigilant.

Lucky was enjoying himself now, growing in confidence that he had been right all along about his passengers' cautiousness, and expecting to have the last laugh. He would never let them live it down, he decided. Every time they saw a Vulcan he would ask whether they wanted to take a detour in case it was following them, he thought, chuckling to himself. And he would make a habit of looking anxiously over his shoulder…

'Look! There it is!' cried Sophie. She had spotted the white Vulcan in a small car park on the edge of the forest. Before Lucky had the chance to take this in he realised there was a man standing in the road directly in his path. Instinctively he braked, but as the car slowed to a halt the man raised his right arm, pointed a gun and fired at the car. The shot hit the front windscreen, but failed to penetrate the bulletproof glass. Instantly, Lucky's foot hit the accelerator and the sports car hurtled towards the man. He was slow to react and did not manage to get clear of the road. Phil grabbed the steering wheel in an attempt to avoid the collision but Lucky's grip was firm. The front corner of the car struck the attacker's legs and knocked him into the air. He tumbled down the passenger side of the car. In the fraction of a second during which he fell past the window Sophie caught a glimpse of the agonised look on his face and she screamed. Lucky brought the vehicle to a standstill.

'What the hell were you playing at?' he growled at Phil. The bodyguard did not stop to answer, however. He was out of the car in a flash, running back to the assailant. The man was alive and writhing around on the edge of the road. Phil approached swiftly, but cautiously. The attacker had dropped his gun; nevertheless Phil was wary in case he had another weapon, or in case he had booby-trapped his body. Lucky reversed the Ultramobile towards them and got out. Phil's attention was focused on the wounded gunman. Clearly he was in no condition to resist. It was obvious that both his legs were broken. He was groaning loudly and calling for help. While Phil was satisfying himself that it was safe to attend to the man Lucky began hunting around in the road. As Phil began to examine the man's injuries, he became vaguely aware that Lucky had picked something up and was walking towards them. Lucky glanced up and down the road in both directions. There was no sign of any traffic in either direction. Phil was crouching over the wounded man's legs.

'We need to dial 999: have you got your mobile?' he began, without looking up, but even as he spoke Lucky was pointing something down at the man. Sophie, who had been looking on in horror from the car, suddenly realised what was happening.

'No, Dad, don't!' she shrieked, but it was too late. There were three loud bangs in quick succession and the prostrate figure on the roadside shuddered as each shot penetrated his chest. Phil made an attempt to grab the gun, but Lucky dodged his outstretched hand and held on to the weapon.

'You're crazy!' Phil cried. He looked back down at the body in the road, now obviously lifeless. Then he turned again and looked Lucky in the eye. Even in the darkness which now prevailed he could see the mixture of venom and satisfaction. Sophie's hysterical crying reached them from the car and complemented the ugliness of this sight.

'Vermin,' Lucky declared, still staring down at the dead man. He went to throw the weapon away, then thought better of it.

'Help me get him into the boot,' Lucky ordered suddenly.

Phil did not respond, but looked on in stunned silence.

'I said help me get him into the boot,' Lucky commanded him, more loudly. He still had the gun in his right hand, and Phil sensed his grip was tightening on it. Ironically, since it had come to light that the death threat was false, Phil was no longer entitled to carry his own weapon and he now realised he was defenceless in the presence of a madman with a gun. Keeping an eye on Lucky the whole time, Phil reluctantly assisted with the transfer of the body to the boot of the Ultramobile. Sophie's sobs turned to wails as she realised what was happening.

Remarkably, no other vehicles had appeared from either direction throughout the incident. Lucky had just restarted the car when a tractor and a convoy of cars trailing it came towards them. It seemed that yet again Hanson's good fortune might enable him to go unpunished.

They travelled back to *Paradise* without speaking. Lucky kept the gun between his seat and the door of the vehicle, more than a little wary of Phil now. Eventually Sophie managed to control her grief, and she sat, motionless except for a slight trembling of the hands, her body rigid with the tension. As they reached *Paradise* and the gates opened a sound from the rear of the vehicle gave them all a start. The attacker's mobile phone was ringing. They listened as *Grande Valse* played merrily. Sophie found herself mumbling a prayer – a prayer born of desperation rather than conviction. She prayed that by some miracle she might hear the assailant answering the phone. The tones rang off and there was silence.

Lucky stopped the vehicle at the foot of the steps and they all got out. Phil noticed that Lucky still had the gun in his hand. The Ultramobile, with the body still in the boot, set off in the direction of its garage, the door to which began to open. As they watched it trundle away they heard the mobile phone ringing again. This time Sophie made no attempt to reiterate the prayer which had previously gone unanswered.

Chapter 18

There was little conversation in *Paradise* that evening. Sophie, still in a deep state of shock, poured herself a large glass of martini, downed it quickly, and immediately replenished her glass. She stayed on her own in the lounge, curled up in a ball of grief on the sofa. She refrained from putting the light on, preferring to remain in darkness. Phil looked in and asked whether there was anything he could do for her. She told him there wasn't and he disappeared into his room. Lucky stayed in the television room all evening. The sound of the television filtered through to the lounge: Sophie was vaguely aware that he was channel-hopping more than he usually did. She wondered whether even he might be having trouble coming to terms with what he had done. Around ten o'clock Sophie's turmoil was disturbed when she heard Phil's voice coming from further along the corridor:

'I don't want anything more to do with this,' he began. 'I'm leaving in the morning.'

'Fine,' Lucky replied. 'It's not as though I need a bodyguard now, is it?' he added. Neither man spoke again; the next sound Sophie heard was that of Phil's footsteps as he ascended the staircase.

Shortly afterwards Sophie hauled herself up and staggered along to the television room. Despite her trauma she had managed to think rationally. She had concluded there was only one thing to be done. The truth had to be told. She would have to persuade her father to inform the police.

Lucky was watching the nightly news as she opened the door. Looking up, he noticed her blotchy cheeks and dishevelled hair and looked irritated.

'I wouldn't cry too many tears over that scumbag if I were you, Sophie. I doubt whether he was going to take pity on you once he had done away with me.'

'But why did you have to kill him?' she sobbed.

Lucky shook his head:

'Vermin,' he remarked. 'I just did the world a big favour.'

'Dad, you've got to come clean and tell the police what has happened. I'll stick by you. I'll tell them that he fired the first shot, and that you were in shock when you did what you did. They might not even put you in prison. If they do, I'll come and see you every day, I promise. If you don't tell them, this will always be hanging over us. Even if you manage to get away with it, we'll never be able to forget about what happened. It will be like having a ghost haunting us all day, every day.'

Lucky shook his head again:

'You'll forget about it in time,' he assured her, and his gaze returned to the giant television screen. Immediately his face dropped, prompting Sophie to turn her head in the direction of the screen.

For some seconds they both stared in disbelief at what they saw. Lucky had had a good look at the attacker's face, whereas Sophie had caught only a fleeting glimpse of it. Nevertheless, both recognised the features in the video images with which they were confronted. Lucky pressed the remote control so that they could hear the newscaster's voice:

'The murder took place around two o'clock near the town of Ingleton in Yorkshire. The victim, Peter Follett, is known to have been a police informer during the 1970s. The assailant is believed to be in his late fifties, tall, well built, with grey hair. The victim was married, with three grown-up children.'

As the newscaster moved on to the next item, Lucky looked at Sophie:

'Like I said, I just did the world a favour.'

At first, Sophie did not reply. She was still taking in this latest instalment in the tale of woe in which she had become entangled. Her father got up, went to the kitchen, and put the kettle on. After a few moments she followed him into the room.

'If you're so sure you've done the world a favour, you should be able to persuade the police about that, shouldn't you?'

Lucky turned and looked directly at her; the look on his face suggested his aggravation was growing.

'Look here, Sophie, I am not going to tell the police. That jerk got what he asked for. I'll get rid of the body and we can get on with our lives in peace.'

'What makes you so sure you won't get caught?'

'I never get caught.'

Sophie hesitated for a moment, summoning up her resolve. Then she continued:

'Dad, if you don't tell the police, I will.'

Lucky's eyes flashed in anger for a moment, then he regained his composure.

'So you would land your own father in it, would you?'

He walked over to the kitchen table, picked up the cordless phone, and came and stood right by her.

'Well, if you're going to do it, at least have the decency to do it front of me.' He held out the phone to her. 'Here,' he began softly, 'I won't try to stop you.'

Sophie took the phone. She dialled the first nine, then the second, and placed her finger on the requisite digit for the third time. She allowed it to hover over the key for a few seconds, but somehow could not bring herself to exert the pressure required to complete the number.

'Damn it, Dad!' she cried out, slammed the phone down on the table, turned and ran from the room.

Chapter 19

Midnight arrived. There was silence in *Paradise,* but a tumult raged within Sophie's mind. After the abortive attempt to call the police she had gone straight to bed, knowing in her heart that her prospects of going to sleep were remote. She heard her father go to bed shortly afterwards. Phil had not reappeared and she presumed he had turned in for the night. The need to talk to someone – anyone at all really, except her father – became overwhelming. Sophie got up, went to put on a dressing gown, and then realised that she hadn't even bothered to undress. She tiptoed along to Phil's room and tapped on the door. There was no answer. She knocked a little louder, but there was still nothing. She listened carefully and realised that she could just about hear him snoring. Sophie wondered whether to wake him up. It crossed her mind that this might not be a good idea. He might be jumpy and would have been trained to defend himself against intruders. Deciding to risk it, she turned the handle and pushed, but it didn't yield. Phil must have locked the door.

It occurred to Sophie to try calling William. Keeping quiet in case she disturbed her father, she went back downstairs. After pouring herself another martini, she retrieved the portable phone from the kitchen and carried both it and the glass back up to her bedroom. Within a couple of minutes she had finished off the martini. She continued to contemplate the possibility of making the call. If she did, she would have to tell him that something was wrong. He would know that immediately from her voice. If she told him what was wrong, she would be putting him in the same predicament she had faced: inform the police and bring her father to account for his actions, or keep quiet and become an accessory to what he had done. Her imagination began to work on some other possibilities. She could say she was calling to beg his forgiveness for the incident in the pool, or she could say she had watched some distressing programme on the television. Or she could say she had had a nightmare…

Yes, she could pretend that she had just dreamed about the ordeal at the Burkins. That would be quite plausible. After all the impact of the two experiences was very similar, except that the one which she had endured yesterday was somehow even worse, and the consequences of her father's actions threatened to linger indefinitely. She wondered whether she could maintain the pretence if she told William it was just a nightmare. After all, she might continue to be traumatised for the rest of her life…If she spoke to William, she would have to admit the truth sooner or later. The only solution would be to persuade her father to come clean in the meantime. And she was going to have to do that anyway…

With quivering fingers she dialled William's number. Again she found herself hesitating before applying the pressure required to complete this task. This time, however, she managed to summon up the necessary courage. She held the handset to her ear and listened for the phone to start ringing. The moment it did the anxiety returned and after the second tone she rang off. She would leave the rest to fate, she decided. If William or his parents had heard the phone ringing, they would be able to tell that it was her number and return the call if they wanted. Otherwise she would just leave it and deal with this situation herself. She remained motionless, desperately yearning for the purring sound which would indicate that her cry for help was being answered. She imagined William stirring in his bed, wondering who could possibly be calling at this hour, realising it must be an emergency, and making his way downstairs to the phone in the hallway. She visualised him picking up the handset, checking what number the call had been made from, and realising that it was hers. Would his heart miss a beat? Would he press the 'return call' button with a trembling hand? Or would he simply replace the handset and return to bed? Had he already consigned her and everything they had shared to the past? If he had, then perhaps he had inadvertently done himself a favour, she reasoned. Her life would certainly never be the same again, and he would have avoided becoming embroiled in the mess which her father had created.

A couple of minutes had passed since she rang off. Sophie reminded herself that William was a heavy sleeper. She remembered Imogen had said that he took after his father in that respect. In all probability neither William nor Dudley would have heard the phone ringing. However Imogen might have heard it. If she had, she would surely have come downstairs and checked the number. She too would have recognised it, and normally she would have rung back at once. But it occurred to Sophie that William must have put his parents in the picture about how things stood between them, and that even Imogen's tolerance and understanding might have been exhausted when she became aware of Sophie's revelation.

Giving up hope on the idea of her call being returned, Sophie lay down and tried to contemplate the possibility of sleep. Sooner or later, she told herself, she would have to be calm enough to doze off. She tried putting the light off, but now the darkness yielded new horrors. Her mind's eye conjured up ugly compilations of memories of the previous day. The tortured face falling past the window of the Ultramobile, her father firing the shots into the prostrate figure in the road, the eerie video images of the attacker caught just a few hours beforehand making his getaway from the murder scene. There was something worrying her about this last image. She couldn't put her finger on it, but she had suspected at the time that there was something not quite right about it.

Switching the lamp back on, Sophie tried to concentrate on recalling what it was that had struck her at the time of the news report. She hoped that at least this would distract her from the gruesome memories which were flickering away in her mind, although less vividly now that she had opened her eyes again. She discounted the possibility that it was something to do with the visual evidence. The attacker's face was too obviously similar, and Lucky had immediately recognised it too. There simply had to be a connection. So, what was it that didn't make sense? Was it something the newsreader had said? Sophie went back over what she could remember...Peter Follett...a police informer...a town in Yorkshire, the name of which escaped her...the description of the assailant, all of which made sense when applied to the body now beginning to rot in the garage. No, it was nothing to do with any of those things. She determined to keep going until she had remembered. Sophie felt sure that there was something extremely important about it, and that if she failed to get to the bottom of it then there would be yet another bizarre twist to this already incredible series of events. She decided to switch on her own television set and wait for a news broadcast in the hope that the report would be shown again.

The late night television programmes would not have been of interest to her under normal circumstances. Now, however, she tried to use them as a means of keeping her mind away from what had happened. The effect was that she was lulled into an uneasy state of partial alertness.

At times she was sufficiently awake to flick through the channels in search of a news broadcast, but there seemed to be a total absence of late night bulletins. She checked the time: it was two o'clock. And that was when it dawned on her...the newscaster had said that the attack in Yorkshire had occurred at just after two o'clock in the afternoon. That gave the attacker just three hours to get from Yorkshire to Sussex. Sophie knew that such a journey would take about five or six hours by car, and still longer by train. She pondered how he could have covered the distance in that time. Could he have travelled by private plane or helicopter, she wondered? But why arrange such a tight schedule between the attacks? Maybe murderers were irrational people, who behaved in inexplicable ways, she concluded.

Then she remembered something else, which cast even more doubt on the plausibility of the scenario she had envisaged. If she had been right in thinking that the attacker had been following them in the Vulcan before they had arrived at the pub, he would have needed to have made his way to Sussex and begun to tail them by about half past three. It simply wasn't possible. Perhaps the newscaster had been mistaken about the time, she thought. Yes, maybe that was the explanation. She decided she would have to check the newspaper in the morning and see what it had to say about the timing of the murder. So she switched off the television, turned out the light, and made another attempt at getting to sleep.

Her contemplations must have done her some good for within a few minutes Sophie had succumbed to her exhaustion. However her slumbers were fitful and her dreams contained haunting visions. Her subconscious must have continued her deliberations, because suddenly she found herself sitting bolt upright in bed. Her heart was pounding and she was covered in perspiration. Despite the fact that nobody was there to listen, she gave voice to the solution which had mysteriously sprung to mind, in a single word:

'Twins.'

Sophie nodded as she spoke. She lay back and considered this possibility. The more she thought about it, the more convinced she became that it was plausible. If one twin had carried out the attack in Yorkshire while the other had ambushed them it would explain the unmistakable resemblance while removing the problem with the timing. Also, it tied in with something that she remembered William had mentioned. During their walk in St. Leonard's forest he had told her that it had occurred to him while on holiday that what he had actually seen at the Burkins' was two very similar attackers, rather than the same man before and afterwards as he had first thought.

So who were these twins who had gone on this killing spree and what were their motives, she wondered? Common to most of the attacks was an association with the Walton Foundation, which suggested they were fanatical protesters. But Peter Follett was said to have been a police informer in the 1970s – the same period during which her father had been involved in crime. She had no recollection of either her father or any other member of the family mentioning twin brothers, but if they were criminal associates it was unlikely that anyone would have talked about them in front of her.

Sophie's train of thought faltered and she found herself becoming tearful and tense. She decided to force herself to concentrate on her deliberations, even if she didn't think that she was going to achieve anything as a result. She returned to the supposition that the attacks were related to the world of crime. She knew too little about Dr Walsingham to have any idea as to whether he had any connection with the underworld, although on the face of it this seemed unlikely. As for Henry Burkin, most of what she knew about him had come from her conversations with Anita. She was aware that he had a number of enemies. She knew that some of them were due to his ruthless ambition, but she also recalled that Anita had told her that he had had a girlfriend who had committed suicide when he left her for Melissa, and that the woman concerned came from a large family, which included several brothers. Sophie recollected that Anita had told her that her father had lived in fear of revenge for some time afterwards. She wondered whether the police had investigated this. It was possible that they were totally unaware of this occurrence, given that Henry, Melissa and Anita were all dead. Sophie knew that there were no other close relatives who might have been in a position to help the police. In fact there had been very few relatives at all at the funeral. However, one person who Sophie had been surprised to see there was Dr Braithwaite. She had learned from him that he and Henry Burkin had been at school together. Perhaps he would be able to shed some light on the matter. She resolved to call him in the morning and see if he could help.

Then Sophie remembered something else which might be significant. She recalled that her mother had once mentioned that as a young woman she had had a friend who killed herself when her lover jilted her. It could just be coincidence, of course.

Anyway, there was no way of knowing now. Or was there…?

Sophie got up and opened her bedroom door. She made her way quietly down the corridor, pausing outside Phil's room. She could hear him snoring more loudly now. Sophie carried on towards the far end of the passage, towards the room just short of her father's bedroom, which her mother had used for correspondence and reading. She was about to reach for the door handle when a noise from outside startled her. Turning, she looked out through one of the windows which overlooked the front of the mansion. As the noise stopped, she realised what it was. One of the garage doors had been opened. She could see her father walking towards the garage, carrying a torch. Sophie realised that the garage was the one with the Ultramobile inside. She watched as Lucky went into the garage, and carried on round to the back of the vehicle. Shortly afterwards he re-appeared. Holding the torch in his right hand he examined something small he was holding in his left hand. She couldn't quite make out what it was. Lucky walked back to the entrance to the mansion, but soon returned; the door to the garage which housed the Ultramobile closed and the one beside it opened. Lucky went inside and moments later Wednesday's car emerged. The garage door closed behind it and seconds later the vehicle disappeared through the gates of *Paradise*.

Sophie guessed where he was going – where all murderers were said to go: back to the scene of the crime. Her heart sank as she confronted the awful truth. Her father was a murderer. Admittedly, he was not the sort of murderer who had plotted his crimes. Nor had he acted without provocation, it was true. Nevertheless, there had been a moment in time when he had been given the choice as to whether or not to take a human life, and he had found within him whatever degree of callousness was required to perform the dreadful deed. Sophie wondered whether anyone had discovered evidence of what had occurred yet: she couldn't help hoping that they had, and that her father would be caught red-handed at the scene of the crime. She knew this was unlikely, however. Perhaps her father was right. He would be able to cover up the crime, dispose of the body, and get away with it. Perhaps he was destined to avoid being punished for all his misdemeanours. Perhaps he really was lucky.

As she stood in the corridor, still gazing aimlessly out of the window, Sophie was moved to ask herself whether there were any circumstances in which she might act with the same ruthlessness that he had shown. After all, she was his daughter. Might she not have inherited the monstrous element of his character in some way which hadn't come to light yet? She shuddered at the thought. Then, from nowhere, she heard the reassuring sound of her mother's voice: 'No, you're much more like me.' And somehow Sophie managed a smile.

Chapter 20

There was enough light filtering through the gap in the curtains to enable Sophie to find the little table lamp which sat on top of the old wooden bureau. Her mother had preferred this lamp to the light which hung from the ceiling, saying that it gave the room a cosier atmosphere in which to write. Iris had often come here at dusk to enter her recollections of the day's events in her diary, or to attend to correspondence with friends and pen friends. Sophie had persuaded her father to leave the room just as it was when her mother died, although in fact she had rarely entered it since, finding that the memories the experience brought back were too painful.

She crossed the room to the bureau and opened it a little tentatively, not having done so since shortly after her mother's death. The passage of time had enabled even Sophie's vivid memory to relinquish its grasp on the detail of the bureau's contents. She had forgotten the photograph album on which her eyes alighted. Opening it up, she was taken back to a time when her world was a very different and altogether far more palatable one. There were souvenirs of the last holiday she had spent with her parents and grandfather. Smiling faces were set against a backdrop of green undulations with hints of splendid sunsets. Southern Ireland, August 2003: Sophie had just met William for the first time. Although she had made no plans to see him again, indeed they hadn't even exchanged phone numbers, some instinct had alerted her to the fact that someone special had arrived. The exuberance this had generated had added an extra dimension to the holiday, making it one of the highlights of her entire life. There had been a wonderful entwinement of peace and exhilaration during that week. She looked right through the whole album. The last photograph had been taken by the waitress as they raised their glasses prior to their evening meal on the final day of their stay. Sophie remembered dreaming of William as her grandfather had proposed a toast *'to a happy and healthy future for us all.'*

As Sophie closed the album the awful irony of her grandfather's words hit home to her. Within a year his life had been ended by a massive stroke; his demise was as sudden as that of his daughter the following summer. And now her father had done an unspeakable deed which could never be rectified, her relationship with William was in tatters, and in this, her hour of need, she had no one to turn to. The grief that she had managed to suppress during her deliberations suddenly overwhelmed her and she caved in. Sophie found herself gasping for breath; unable to add volume to her wailing, she emitted high-pitched pining sounds, whimpering helplessly like an abandoned baby.

At length this torment passed and the reason for her visit to this room came back to her. She opened the bottom drawer of the bureau and took out the box marked 'correspondence received'. Sophie knew that her mother had kept every letter she had been sent by friends, and that they were well organised, being filed according to sender and in chronological order. Some correspondents could be ruled out straight away, since they had come to know Iris later on in her life. Sophie sifted through the remaining writers and took out the letters which derived from the days when her mother was a young adult. There were some thirty letters in all. Sophie looked through each in turn, scanning them for some hint of a reference to her friend's suicide, hoping at least to discover her name. Sophie realised it was unlikely that there would be any indication as to whether the friend had twin brothers. However, she had made up her mind to try, and at least it was a means of focusing on something other than her trauma.

The little cuckoo clock on the wall had just informed her that it was seven o'clock in the morning when Sophie put the last of the letters back in the box. She had found just one potentially helpful comment: a cousin who had emigrated to New Zealand had written that she was 'very sorry to hear about Sarah'. At least she had a possible name with which to attempt to jog Dr Braithwaite's memory. Sophie returned the box to the drawer, then stood up and turned to go. Her gaze fell on the shelf which contained the row of cassettes which had not been played since her mother's death: Simon and Garfunkel, Abba, Elton John, Phil Collins, The Corrs…At the end of the line was an unmarked cassette. That was strange, she thought. Her mother had always made sure that everything was clearly labelled and easily located. Perhaps it had not been touched. She picked it out, and opened the case. No, the tape had been used. She could see that from the amount around the spools. Curiosity got the better of her. Sophie inserted the cassette in the portable stereo which she had given her mother on that last Christmas Day together, and which still sat on the small table below the shelf. Sophie rewound the cassette to the beginning of side one. Then she pressed the play button and waited.

Chapter 21

Lucky glanced furtively around as he approached the Vulcan. He was concerned about leaving footprints at the scene, but to his relief the car park was not muddy. His gloved hand felt around in his coat pocket. Pulling out the key he had retrieved from the body in the boot of the Ultramobile he opened the driver's door and shone the torch around inside. There was nothing of any consequence. He checked under the sun visor and in the compartment in the side of the door. Again, there was no sign of anything which would yield any clues as to the driver's intentions. He went round to the passenger side and conducted a similarly thorough examination. He checked the glove compartment for maps, instructions, or correspondence – anything which might link the vehicle to him. A quick search of the rear of the Vulcan was sufficient to satisfy him that there was nothing incriminating within. Finally he checked the boot of the car. He rummaged around amidst the oil cans, jump leads and tins of de-icer until he was certain of the all clear.

Daylight was just beginning to break. Lucky locked the doors of the Vulcan and hurried to the entrance of the car park. He waited for a couple of vehicles to pass before jogging down the road to the scene of the ambush. As he had driven by he had noticed a stile on the opposite side of the road, over which he would be able to climb if any traffic came along. As luck would have it, it had rained during the night, and there were no obvious traces of blood on the road. Lucky shone the torch up and down a few times, trying to make sure that neither he nor Phil had dropped anything. At one point a car could be heard approaching about half a mile away. Lucky had ample time to make it to the cover of the adjacent field and he allowed the vehicle to pass before returning to his quest.

Having satisfied himself that there were no obvious signs of what had occurred the previous day, Lucky made his way back to his car. Passing the car park entrance, he glanced in the direction of the Vulcan. It had crossed his mind to move it away from the scene of the incident, but he was too concerned about leaving forensic evidence behind. He had taken a big enough risk as it was. However he had at least made certain there was nothing at the scene which would incriminate him. As Lucky started the engine he couldn't help feeling a little irritated. The body was still in the boot of the Ultramobile. He would have to find some way of getting rid of it. And then he would have to decide what to do with his precious sports car. The impact with the gunman had caused some damage to the front of the vehicle. It would be too risky to get that repaired; it was too obvious that the vehicle had hit someone. For the same reason he dared not drive it as it was, or try to sell it. Lucky concluded that he would probably have to leave it in the garage indefinitely. That way he could be certain that nobody would suspect anything. Lucky sighed with regret at the fact that he had been driving his favourite car at the time. If only it had been a Wednesday…today's vehicle was the least valuable and had caused him lots of problems. Well, it couldn't be helped. In any case, Lucky had realised that he had a more urgent problem to attend to if he wanted this to be kept quiet. He was confident he could prevent Sophie from telling anyone, but Phil was another matter. As he journeyed back to *Paradise* Lucky considered his options. Money might be the answer, he concluded, and a pledge to continue the treatment. Or he could threaten to make counter-accusations if Phil went to the police. One thing was certain. He couldn't risk leaving it to chance. He would certainly have to do something.

Imogen placed her hand on her son's shoulder as she passed behind him. William was seated at the breakfast table, staring into his bowl of cornflakes.

'Oh come on, cheer up!' Imogen implored him softly. William looked apologetic and smiled half-heartedly up at her. 'For goodness sake, call her,' his mother went on. Before

William had had the chance to reply, Dudley came into the room. Never at his best in the mornings, his grey hair was ruffled and his eyes were not fully open.

'Did I hear the phone ring in the middle of the night?' he wanted to know.

'I didn't hear anything,' William responded.

Imogen picked up the portable handset and pressed the requisite digits.

They watched her face as it started to show concern.

'That's Sophie's number,' she began. 'At twelve twenty a.m.' She put the phone down on the table close to William. 'That's not normal. She would never ring that late unless something was wrong.'

William nodded.

'I think you should call her,' Imogen declared.

William sighed, and did not respond.

Something about William's refusal to acknowledge the situation spurred Imogen into action. She became at once passionate and lucid.

'Listen, William, if you don't ring her, I will. And for heaven's sake, stop sitting there looking so sorry for yourself. Sophie's a wonderful girl. It would be amazing if you ever found anyone else like her. And she adores you. If you can't see that, well, more fool you. And as for what happened while you were away, well, if you hadn't been so insensitive before you went, it would never have occurred. Anyway, nothing actually happened. And Sophie's had the courage to come clean and tell you.' She paused for a moment, wringing her hands together with the effort of concentration, before continuing:

'Look, your holiday made you realise how you felt about her. And when she thought that it was your spaceship which crashed, that made her realise how she felt about you. It's obvious; it was meant to happen like that. You and Sophie belong together. So if you know what's good for you, take her back.'

William looked up at his mother. He nodded again, more positively this time.

'I'll ring her,' he promised.

'Thank goodness for that.'

'It's a bit early at the moment,' he added. 'It's only half past seven. Sophie doesn't usually get up until about nine o'clock.'

Imogen went to protest, then hesitated. She looked across at Dudley, in a manner which suggested that she wanted his opinion.

'It can't have been that important, or else she would have rung back,' he asserted.

'I'll ring her,' William repeated, 'at nine o'clock.'

'Okay,' Imogen agreed, and as she sat down beside him she breathed a sigh of relief.

Chapter 22

There was silence at first: perhaps the cassette was blank after all, Sophie thought. She placed her finger over the 'stop' button, and then hesitated. What was that faint noise in the background? She moved her hand to the volume control. A few seconds passed by without any further sound, so she stopped the tape, rewound it, and listened again. There! This time she knew what the noise was. Sophie recognised the sound of her mother, clearing her throat. She waited, fervently hoping for something more. The seconds she knew would be silent passed by, testing her patience. All at once that unmistakable voice came flooding out of the speakers:

'Hello, Sophie, oh my precious Sophie! I feel so sad today! Can you hear it in my voice? I'm sure you can. Oh, I do so hope I'm wrong! It's just that I have this feeling I can't explain. I know you sometimes get them too. What is it you call them? Something beginning with "I". Ah yes, "intuitions", that's it. Well, I have an intuition that something terrible is going to happen to me soon. I don't know what it is, but I have been coming over all queer recently. I just feel that somehow I haven't got long for this world. If you are listening to this, then you'll know I was right. Oh, Sophie, I only hope it isn't going to happen. I don't want to leave you. I'm really not ready to go yet. And I'm worried about you. And your father…Ah, your father, what would you do with him, eh? I just wish he would be more thoughtful. Oh Sophie, I've never really admitted it to anyone, but you see…oh, this is hard to tell you…you see, your father and I…we were never really in love…not like it's meant to be. It's just, more than anything else I wanted a child, and he was there, wanting to marry me. It was all so sudden, and just as I was beginning to give up hope…I thought it might be my last chance, so you see, I said yes…Oh, I wonder if I did the right thing…If it wasn't for you, my wonderful daughter, I would say it was wrong…If I had known about his past, I mean about the things he was involved in, it might have been different…perhaps it was as well I didn't know…you see, I wouldn't say your father's a bad man, oh no, it's just that he does some very foolish things sometimes…and I worry that one day he's going to…well, do something he'll really regret. While I'm around I can keep an eye on him, but if I'm not…Oh Sophie, you must look after yourself, you really must, and watch him closely…otherwise I'm sure it's just a matter of time…before he does…do something.' There was a pause, and then her mother's voice sounded again, more quietly this time:

'Sophie, nobody knows I'm making this tape. It's just for you. Keep it somewhere safe. I have more things to say to you. I can hear your father out in the corridor, so I had better go. I'll finish this tomorrow…'

There was silence, except for the gentle hissing sound which occurs when the tape has not been used. Sophie waited for more, but as the seconds ticked by her hope that her mother had been able to conclude her message faded. Now she knew why the cassette had not been left at the beginning. Sophie waited while the tape finished, and then sampled enough of the other side to satisfy herself that it was blank. It was unlike her mother to leave something unfinished, she reflected. In particular, Iris's concluding remark that she would finish 'tomorrow' suggested very strongly that the tape had been made on the last morning of her life.

The sickening irony struck Sophie. For years the cassette had been sitting there untouched, leaving her in ignorance of the message of warning about her father. Might it have made some difference if she had been aware of its existence the previous morning? Might she have acted differently, perhaps by being more insistent that they went home by an alternative route, or by getting out of the Ultramobile at the same time as her father in order to keep an eye on him? She would never know now. As for the revelation about the circumstances in which her mother and father had come together, this came as no surprise. In fact, she had known in her heart that theirs was not a marriage made in heaven.

Sophie noticed the daylight. She had barely had a wink of sleep that night. Perhaps this was why she felt so numb, she thought. Her mind still hadn't taken in what had happened and she felt emotionally drained. Her body was weary and she had to force herself to get up and go back to her room to retrieve the portable handset. As she passed Phil's room, she looked in through the now open door. The room was empty. He must have packed and slipped out quietly, she concluded. Moving on, she noticed through the window that Phil was just putting his suitcase in the boot of his car. She watched as the gates opened. He turned right at the bottom of the drive as on any other morning. Sophie wondered whether he would visit the gym as usual before deciding what to do next. Poor Phil, she thought. How unfortunate that things should have turned so sour, so suddenly. She hoped that he would get in contact to let her know what had happened to him, although she suspected that it was unlikely that he would think to do this.

As Sophie stood contemplating she thought she heard her father's voice coming from downstairs. She went to the top of the stairs. She caught the last few words of the phone conversation he had been having: 'Yeah...all right...I'll go and check.... I'll see you back here...okay, mate.'

Sophie heard the front door slam. Returning to the window, she watched as Lucky hurried out to the garages. In an instant Wednesday's car was speeding down the drive. Sophie did not stop to watch it disappear. Now was her chance to find out what Dr Braithwaite knew. Somehow she felt sure that he would be able to shed some light on what lay behind the attacks, and that this would enable her to convince her father to go to the police. As she returned to her room, a disturbing thought crossed Sophie's mind. What if Dr Braithwaite was in some way connected with the murders? After all, he knew Dr Walsingham, Henry Burkin, and her father. Then she remembered his soft voice, his calm and gentle demeanour, and his obvious benevolence. No, she thought, there's no way he could ever hurt anyone. So she dismissed the thought as readily as it occurred to her, picked up the portable handset and rang Directory Enquiries for the number for the Walton Foundation.

The receptionist put her on hold for a minute; Dr Braithwaite had only just arrived at the clinic and was still making his way to his office. Sophie was still contemplating what to say when he picked up the receiver:

'Good morning, Dr Braithwaite speaking.'

'Hello, Dr Braithwaite, I don't know if you remember me – Sophie Hanson.'

'Yes of course, my dear. I'm sorry I missed you yesterday. I was at a conference. Tell me, have you changed your mind about coming here?'

'Oh, no, that's not why I'm ringing.' Sophie was conscious that her voice sounded croaky and cleared her throat in the hope of disguising her distress.

'What's the matter, my dear? You sound terrible,' the doctor observed.

'Oh, I've hardly slept. It's just…' Sophie found her hold on her emotions beginning to fail. And she sensed that here, at last, was someone she could talk to.

'What is it, my dear? Has something happened?' Sophie could tell his concern was genuine.

'If I tell you, will you promise not to say anything to anyone, unless I say so?'

The doctor hesitated for a moment. Instinct told him that what she was about to impart was extremely significant, and it occurred to him he might regret making such a promise.

'Tell me what's wrong,' he requested, hoping to avoid being put on the spot. Sophie was not going to be deflected, however:

'I need you to promise,' she asserted.

'Very well,' the doctor replied, 'I promise.'

'We were attacked on the way home.'

'Oh no, were you hurt?'

'No, I'm okay.'

'And your father?'

'He…he's all right too. But…he killed the attacker.'

'Oh dear…oh dear, oh dear.' There was a pause while the doctor struggled to comprehend what he was hearing.

Sophie remembered the reason for her call.

'Dr Braithwaite, I'm trying to persuade my father to give himself up.'

'Yes, that would be best.'

'And I want to know who the people behind all this are. You see I'm certain there's more than one person. In fact, I believe there are twin brothers involved here. That's what I wanted to ask you. Do you know of any brothers who would have had a grudge against Dr Walsingham?'

Dr Braithwaite thought for a moment:

'No, I can't think of anyone. The police asked me for a list of people Giles had refused to treat. There weren't many people on it and they were all for genuine reasons. I believe the police eliminated them all. I'm sure there weren't any brothers on the list.'

Disappointed, Sophie turned to her other line of enquiry.

'What about Henry Burkin? Did he have a girlfriend who killed herself?'

'Yes, that's right, he did. Why?'

'Was her name Sarah?'

'Yes, I do believe it was.'

'Did she have any brothers?'

Dr Braithwaite scratched his head as he tried to recall. At last he answered:

'She came from a big family. Yes, she had brothers, but I don't know whether there were any twins among them.'

Sophie sighed. She had been hoping for something more concrete.

Dr Braithwaite checked his watch.

'Listen, my dear, I have to go. I'm due to see a client. I do hope you manage to get your father to see sense. I'll give some thought to what you've said and if I can help any further I will.'

Sophie thanked him, but as she rang off she felt her spirits sinking. Somehow she had convinced herself that the conversation would prove more fruitful. A deep anxiety began to overtake her. She wondered whether she was clutching at straws. Even if she managed to uncover something, why should her father change his mind? It was going to fall to her to resolve this once and for all. Either she would have to inform the police herself, or she would have to keep quiet and live with the dreadful knowledge of what happened until such time as the truth came to light. But what if it never came to light? She shuddered at the thought. Would she have to spend her whole life trying to suppress the awareness that there was a corpse gradually decomposing in one of the garages? Desperation began to play tricks on her mind. What if she went out to check, just in case the man was still alive in the boot of the Ultramobile? Why didn't she call the police now and tell them she was ringing on behalf of her father? She could get them to come round while he was out and make out that he had intended to tell them everything on his return. Then when he did come back he would have no choice. At least that way it would seem as though he had decided to own up, which would be better for him than if she reported it herself. What if she threatened to take an overdose if he didn't confess? What if…?

She realised with a start that the portable phone which she was still cradling was ringing.

'Hello,' she managed to say; her voice was even more subdued now.

'Sophie, it's Dr Braithwaite again.'

'Ah, hello,' she said pathetically.

'Listen, my dear, I've remembered some things which may be important. The first was that a few weeks ago my personal assistant told me that a man had rung, saying he was your father's bodyguard. He wanted assurance that the security provisions here were adequate. She told him they were, of course. Then he said your father had asked him to check on the date of his next appointment. She confirmed that he was due to come in yesterday. Does that sound like a genuine call?'

'Well, my father did employ a bodyguard and he was very thorough. It wouldn't surprise me if he had rung you to check on the security arrangements. But as far as asking for the date is concerned, I doubt it. Dad always leaves all that sort of thing to me. If these people had been watching us, they would have known about the fact that Dad had a bodyguard. It's my guess that they made the call in order to plan the ambush. After all, they must have known somehow that we were coming here yesterday.'

Dr Braithwaite was taken aback.

'Oh dear, if that's the case I'm afraid we have inadvertently helped them. I'm very sorry.'

Sophie wanted to reassure him, but words failed her. The doctor continued:

'The other thing I remembered was that the list I provided for the police only contained the names of those people Giles Walsingham had refused to treat. They didn't ask for those whom Philip Tonbridge had turned down when he was working here. It suddenly struck me that shortly before he died Philip refused to treat some twin brothers who had been mercenaries and prior to that had been involved in serious crime. Although it was Philip who dealt with the application, it was Giles who knew the twins' history and it was on his recommendation that treatment was refused.'

He paused. Sophie was already certain this information was significant.

'What were their names?' she asked.

'I'm afraid that's confidential information, my dear. I really shouldn't disclose that. Let me see…I know what I can do, though. Hold the line for a minute.'

Sophie waited. She could hear his voice in the background, but she could not make out what he was saying. Nor could she hear any reply. Presumably he was using another line to make a call.

When he returned there was a note of urgency in his voice.

'Sophie, I've just spoken to an old friend who also knew Henry Burkin when he was younger. He told me Sarah's surname. It was the same as that of the twins who were refused treatment. He also confirmed that she had brothers who were twins. And he said that years ago they were suspected of having been behind a hit-and-run attempt on Henry's life, although shortly afterwards they were sent to prison for some other offences, and nothing was ever proved.'

'Well, there it is then. That can't possibly be a coincidence.'

'I agree. Sophie, we must put the police in the picture as soon as possible.'

'Yes, I know.'

'Will you do it, or do you want me to?'

'Let me tell my father what we've discovered and let him know that the whole thing is going to come out in the open anyway. I want to give him another chance to be the one to tell the police. If he still won't do it, then I'll ask you to call them.'

'Can you speak to him now?'

'No, I don't know where he is at the moment, but he can't have gone far. He's probably gone back to where it happened again.'

'So are you alone there?' Dr Braithwaite asked anxiously.

'Yes, why?'

'Well, because if there were twin brothers involved, then the surviving twin will almost certainly know what his brother was up to, and he might come after your father.'

The thought instantly filled Sophie with alarm. She had overlooked this possibility altogether. She stood up and carried the phone out into the corridor, so that she could see the main entrance to the estate. She found herself recalling Phil's words: '*You should feel quite safe here*.'

'Sophie, are you still there?' Dr Braithwaite asked anxiously.

‘Yes, I’m okay. I don’t think there’s anything to worry about as long as I’m here,’ she assured him. ‘The estate has the most up-to-date security system. And I’m certainly not going anywhere until my dad gets back.’

Dr Braithwaite sensed that Sophie was not going to be dissuaded.

‘Very well, if you insist. Let me know as soon as you’ve spoken to your father. I really must go now. I’m keeping a client waiting.’

Sophie thanked him and rang off. At least there was going to be an end to this nightmare, she concluded. Deciding to take no chances Sophie made her way to the room from which the security system was controlled. She checked all the screens. There was no cause for concern. Sophie decided to stay there until Lucky returned. She turned the swivel chair to face the screen on which the main entrance could be seen, sat back and waited.

Chapter 23

It was the sound of a car engine starting that brought Sophie out of the uneasy sleep into which sheer exhaustion had allowed her to slip. The sound was not directly audible to her, however: it had been picked up by the security system. A quick glance at the plethora of miniature screens behind her enabled her to establish the location of the vehicle concerned. She could see that it was 'Wednesday's car'. Frantically she tried to remember the whereabouts of the mechanism that Phil had shown her which would enable her to see what was happening on the main screen. By the time she had changed the focus her father's car had disappeared. Sophie could now see that another car which had been concealed by it was still there. She didn't recognise the vehicle, but as she looked closely she could see that there was someone at the wheel, although from that angle she couldn't see who it was. Sophie hesitated a moment, wondering whether to run down to find out who it was and get them to set off in pursuit of her father. However, before she could act, the car started to move. As it swung round towards the screen Sophie got a proper view of the driver. It was the last person in the world she wanted to see. As on that sweltering August day when their paths had last crossed she mouthed his name:

'Jock Pope'.

The vehicle disappeared from the screen. Sophie switched the focus back to the gates at the entrance and watched as the car turned right into the road. She looked back at the smaller screens, just in case there was any sign of anyone else, but there was nothing. Sophie cursed the fact that she had dozed off. Not only had she missed the opportunity to talk to her father, but also there was something else afoot now. She had no idea what it was, but it was a safe assumption that if Jock Pope was involved, it was something sinister. If only she could get through to her father… A thought crossed her mind which for some reason had eluded her before. Had he taken his mobile with him? She picked up the cordless phone and dialled the number, but to her dismay she could just about make out a digital melody coming from downstairs.

Sophie was beginning to feel panicky. Perhaps she should have allowed Dr Braithwaite to contact the police. Should she do that even now? The indecision was agonising. As she stood staring at the main screen an idea occurred to her. Phil had explained to her how everything that was caught on camera was stored on tape and had shown her how to access the recordings. If she could just remember…

It took a few minutes of experimenting with switches and dials before Sophie was able to observe what had occurred. The microphones concealed in the garage walls had picked up the conversation between Lucky and Jock, enabling Sophie to hear every word clearly.

Her father had arrived first and stopped Wednesday's car outside the garage. Shortly afterwards he disappeared for a minute in the direction of the mansion. He must have gone to let Jock in, because his return coincided with the arrival of the other car.

Lucky opened *the* garage and both men went inside. Sophie heard her father open the boot of the Ultramobile. Jock was the first to speak:

'Ugh! What a stench!'

'So do you recognise him?' Lucky wanted to know.

'No, can't say I do.'

The boot closed and the two men reappeared. Jock lit a cigarette before continuing:

'You're gonna have to get shot of him. You can't keep the evidence in the bloody garage!'

'Yeah, but where?'

'I'll take care of that. And I'll make sure the garage is clean.'

Jock opened his car door, took out a road atlas and flicked through the pages until he came to the one he wanted.

'Right, show me where this gym is.'

Lucky looked over him and pointed.

'Just near Billingshurst.'

Jock nodded.

'Yep, I know where that is.'

He closed the atlas and looked directly at Lucky.

'I'll do the whole thing for a cool half million. Pay me once everything's died down.'

Lucky hesitated.

'Take it or leave it. That's bloody cheap, I'll tell you, mate.'

Lucky shook his head.

'It's not the money. It's just...well, it's one thing to get rid of vermin like that...it's another when it's someone you know.'

'Well, you need to make your mind up. How long does he normally spend at the gym?'

'An hour and a half, maybe two.'

'And he's been there how long?'

'About twenty minutes.'

Jock looked agitated.

'I'll need time to make sure the coast is clear, get into the car, and set the trap. It's now or never.'

'I dunno, Jock, there must be some other way.'

'Well, you could always sit around and wait until he decides to shop you, or until he thinks to blackmail you.'

Lucky was still hesitating. Jock held his finger aloft and wagged it as he spoke:

'Hey, remember what Jimmy Corbett used to say – do unto others before they do unto you.'

Lucky nodded slowly:

'Okay, you're right. Do it.'

'Good. Now you need to have an alibi. So go into Horsham, or somewhere where lots of people will see you. Better still, get yourself caught on camera. Go into a Building Society, or something. It's not likely that the fuzz will suspect you of bumping off your own bodyguard, but we don't want to take any chances.'

Jock thought for a moment before continuing:

'They'll probably assume it was someone who wanted to get him out of the way in order to get to you, so you may find the Old Bill wanting to set you up with some protection. All the more reason why we've got to get rid of the body in the garage. Look, I'll make sure everything goes off smoothly, and then I'll come straight back here. We're going to have to work fast. I'll see you back here at about eleven.'

Lucky nodded in agreement and both men went to get into their cars. Just as Lucky was opening the door of his vehicle, Jock voiced a further concern:

'What about Sophie? Are you sure you can trust her?'

'Don't worry. I'll handle Sophie,' came the reply.

This time there was no hesitation: Sophie's index finger pressed the button marked 'nine' three times in quick succession. The anger, fear and dismay which the conversation between her father and Jock had aroused in her combined to leave her in no doubt as to what to do.

She got through to the operator straight away and asked for the police. The phone rang and Sophie waited for a response. Her frustration grew as the tones continued to sound. A minute went by before the monotonous ringing became unbearable, and Sophie held the handset away from her ear, checking every few seconds to see whether there had been any response. Her disbelief mounted as the phone continued to ring. She checked the time: it was nearly nine o'clock. An idea occurred to her: there would surely be time to get a taxi down to the gym and alert Phil to the danger he was facing. Perhaps she could put a stop to Jock's efforts to 'set the trap'. Sophie shuddered to think what that meant, but at least the mention of the car had put her in the picture as to where it would be found. Sophie checked once again: there was still no answer. She rang off and dialled the local taxi firm. Again the phone rang a number of times, but this time she did get a reply. The controller recognised her voice and sensed her anxiety. Throwing caution aside, she reinforced the impression – this was literally a matter of life and death, she said. How long for a taxi to Billingshurst, she begged them? Ten minutes, maybe less, came the reply. Again there was the anguish of indecision. The controller was eager for a response. Forced into a corner, Sophie opted to take the taxi and rang off. Anxious not to waste a moment, she decided to make her way to the entrance to *Paradise*, but before she could put the cordless phone down, it rang. Thinking it might be a response to her call to the emergency services, she answered it:

'Hello,' she said. There was a note of trepidation in her voice.

'Sophie, hi,' said a voice she recognised instantly, but which she somehow failed to identify. Her silence gave this away.

'It's William.' It was obvious he was aghast at having to tell her who he was.

'Oh, William, sorry, hello.' Sophie began to make her way towards the staircase.

'Sophie, what's wrong?'

'I can't tell you now. I haven't time.' She began to go downstairs, then realised she would need to pay for the taxi, and hurried back to her room to get her handbag.

'Why did you ring last night?' William persisted.

'Oh, I really can't explain now. I've got to go. Listen, William, if I were you I would find someone else. I think I must be jinxed.'

'But Sophie, that's nonsense.'

'Is it? Everything's going so terribly wrong for me.' Sophie was on her way down the stairs now. 'I don't want you to be mixed up in it,' she added.

'But Sophie…'

'I've got to go now.' Sophie was opening the front door, and the reception on the cordless phone was fading.

'Goodbye, William,' she concluded. Without waiting for an answer, she left the phone in the porch and started to run down the drive.

As Lucky drove into the car park in Horsham the penny finally dropped. All along he had been certain that the attacks had been linked with the groups protesting against the Walton Foundation. Until the moment early that morning when he had opened the boot of the Ultramobile to obtain the key to the dead man's car. He was sure he had seen the man before, but could not remember where. He had expected Jock to be able to help. After all, most of their enemies were mutual. Now, however, he realised why he hadn't recognised the man. Jock was in prison when in the early eighties he had acted as a getaway driver for the Cartwright brothers. Later he had quarrelled with them and when they were caught he had done a deal with the police whereby he testified against them in return for a suspended sentence. He had expected trouble as a result, but when he later learned that the twins had gone abroad to become mercenaries after their release he had assumed he was safe. Lucky nodded to himself as he stopped the car. Yes, the dead man was one of the Cartwright twins, either Bruce or…Bennie, yes that was the other one's name.

Lucky opened the car door, but just at that moment the same thought which had occurred to Dr Braithwaite struck him. What about the remaining twin? For the first time, Lucky admitted to himself that he felt uncertain about getting out of this situation. Each time he thought he had everything under control something else cropped up. Closing the car door, Lucky remained in the driver's seat and considered the consequences of this latest realisation. His train of thought followed that of Dr Braithwaite: the other twin must have been aware of his brother's intentions and would surely now be attempting to find out what had happened to him. It was likely that his investigations would lead him to *Paradise*. The only thing to do was to be ready for him when he arrived. He would have to speak to Jock about it as soon as they had both got back to the estate, he concluded. Remembering he was supposed to be establishing his alibi for Phil's death, Lucky opened the car door again and got out. He took a few steps, but then stopped abruptly in his tracks. He had overlooked something – something which filled him at once with horror and guilt. The only person he cared about was alone at home, unaware that she may be in grave danger. In an instant Lucky turned round, got back into the car, and began to speed through Horsham town centre. As he did so, he thought he heard a voice inside his head. It was a voice he had forgotten. 'What have you done?' said the voice; anger and despair were entwined in every word. 'What have you done?' it said again, and Lucky remembered how Iris's habit of repeating herself could become quite nauseating when she was nervous or panicky. 'What have you done?' It was beginning to torment him now. Lucky jumped a red light as he turned onto the Brighton Road and hurtled along towards the countryside. 'What have you done?' the voice cried again. 'Oh, shut up!' he retorted aloud. The voice, however, would not go away. 'What have you done, oh Andrew, what have you done? *What have you done*?'

Chapter 24

'Do you know the gym near Billingshurst?' Sophie asked the driver hurriedly.

'Yes, miss,' came the reply.

'Take me there as fast as you possibly can,' she instructed him.

'Very well, miss,' he replied. As he began to turn the car round, he recognised her as the young woman he had taken to the graveyard at Coolhurst a while back. Her behaviour on that occasion had struck him as rather unusual. Now here she was on a mission to a gym which the controller had informed him was 'a matter of life and death.'

The driver was rather dubious about this supposed urgency. He was not about to get caught speeding or take any chances just to keep her happy. He decided he would make out he was putting his foot down, without actually going flat out.

'I'll pay you now, please,' Sophie told him, 'I can't afford to waste a moment once we get there.'

'I don't know how much it will be yet, miss.'

'Well, look, I've got fifty pounds here. It won't be more than that, will it?' Sophie leaned forward, held her hand out, and waited until the driver had the opportunity to remove his left hand from the steering wheel and accept the note. 'Keep the change,' Sophie continued, 'just get me there as soon as you can.'

The driver eyed her curiously in the interior mirror. 'Yes, miss,' he assured her earnestly.

Lucky was travelling too fast to pay much attention to the vehicles coming towards him. He was chancing his arm even more than usual, hell bent on getting back to *Paradise* without wasting a second. He was still trying to suppress the ranting of the accuser within his mind. Taking a bend on the wrong side of the road, Lucky failed to notice the taxi in his path until the last minute. He had to swerve to avoid a collision, and there was no possibility of recognising the occupant in the back of the vehicle. Sophie saw him, however, and for a moment considered asking the driver to turn back. A glance at her watch told her this could be a fatal mistake: her priority had to be to ensure that Phil was safe.

'Bloody maniac,' the driver muttered. Sophie said nothing, being disinclined to contradict him.

As he drove into *Paradise* Lucky glanced furtively around. He had taken little notice of the tuition Phil had given him with respect to the security system, but he did remember that an intruder's presence would set the alarm off. Opening the front door, he was relieved to discover that the system had not been triggered. He was surprised to see the portable handset right by the front door. 'Sophie' he called out. He took a look around on the ground floor. There was no indication that she had come down for breakfast. He hurried upstairs, expecting to find that she had gone back to bed. Without stopping to knock, he opened the door and peered round. Puzzled by the room's emptiness, he stepped back out into the corridor and called his daughter's name again. Noticing that the door to the room which housed the security controls had been left open, he hurried back down the corridor. He was surprised to see that the focus of the main screen had been changed from the entrance to *Paradise* to the garage area. For a moment the significance of the fact that this was where he had conspired with Jock was lost on him. Suddenly, however, everything fell into place. 'She knows,' he said aloud. 'That's where she's gone,' he continued, remembering the near miss with the taxi. He ran along the corridor, and down the stairs. As he did so, he began to weigh up the options available to him. There was no point in trying to persuade her to go along with the plan to kill Phil: she would never have that. He would have to stop Jock from setting the trap, and take a chance on what Phil would do. As he got to the hallway he could hear that the phone was ringing. He grabbed the portable handset, hoping against hope that it might be Jock.

'Hello,' he began anxiously.

The voice was not the one he had wanted to hear:

'Yes, this is the police. There was an emergency call from this number. We've been trying to get back to you, but the phone was engaged.'

Lucky hesitated.

'No,' he said slowly, trying to sound calm.

'Yes, a young lady rang about twenty minutes ago.'

'Well, there's no young lady here. It must be some sort of mistake. Goodbye.' And he put the phone down before the caller could reply.

'Damn!' he cursed aloud. They would probably look into that and he would have to dream up some sort of explanation. There was yet another problem to solve. It would have to wait, though. His first task had to be to get over to the gym. He glanced at his watch: it was 9.20 a.m. A horrifying thought crossed his mind. What if Sophie got caught in the trap which Jock had set for Phil? The voice in his head started up again, screeching hysterical condemnation. Lucky stood petrified, tormented, wasting valuable seconds, until a sound disturbed him – an electronic beep which indicated that there was a vehicle at the entrance to Paradise. Could the police have responded that quickly? Had Jock done the business already? Or had Sophie instructed the taxi driver to turn round for some reason? Lucky checked the screen in the hallway and was surprised to find that it was none of these. It took him a moment before he remembered why the yellow MG was familiar to him. Regaining his focus on the urgency to get to the gym, Lucky made no attempt to stop and let William in. He hurried through the porch; leaving the front door open behind him, he ran down the steps and got back into Wednesday's car. Starting the engine, he somehow managed to remember that the vehicle was almost out of diesel. In an instant an idea occurred to him: he sped down the drive, and as the gates opened he brought the car rapidly to a halt, stopping close to the sports car. William, who was standing between the two cars, got in his way as he tried to get out of the vehicle.

'What's happening? Is Sophie all right?' William demanded.

Lucky ignored him, pushed past, and grabbed the handle of the door to the MG. Realising that Lucky was about to take the car, William tackled him from behind and pulled him to the ground. Surprised by the strength that his determination generated in him, William pinned the older man to the ground, completely subduing him.

Their eyes met. William's anger was apparent; Lucky was beginning to take on the look of a desperate man.

'Let me go!' Lucky pleaded. 'Sophie's in danger.'

'Where is she?' William hissed.

'I'll take you to her,' Lucky gasped, his breathing impaired by the pressure of William's weight.

William released his grasp, and got to his feet.

'I'll drive,' said Lucky as he too got up. 'It'll be quicker.'

William had heard enough from Sophie about her father's style of driving to know better than to dispute this.

Chapter 25

Phil shook his head he looked at the printout which analysed his performance on the rowing machine. He was nowhere near up to speed this morning. He knew very well that this was no reflection on his physical condition. The truth was his attention was elsewhere. He had been forced to reflect on a number of problems which had simply not existed when he last visited the gym twenty-four hours earlier. Finding somewhere to stay was not an immediate difficulty; he knew he could count on his brother to put him up while he sorted himself out. Getting another job was going to prove more complicated; not only would he be hard pushed to find anything which suited him anywhere near as well as the position he had just vacated, but also he would have to explain to prospective employers why he had left so suddenly. And then there was the question of references…he had considered approaching Hanson to give him glowing references in return for his silence about the killing of the man in the road. But his conscience was troubling him about this option. Far from being ready to agree to keep quiet, Phil was beginning to regret that he had not already gone along with the inclination he had had following his brush with Hanson the previous evening to report the incident to the police. Two factors had deterred him. Firstly, he was concerned that he would be implicated in the killing, due to the fact that he had helped put the body in the boot of the Ultramobile – could he count on the police to believe that he had felt that his own life was in danger at that point? Secondly, he felt sorry for Sophie and did not want to be the one to cause her further suffering.

He made his way to the steam room. It happened to be unoccupied, giving him the opportunity to continue his deliberations. For some minutes he sat with his head in his hands, his eyes closed behind his moist palms, as he focused on his dilemma, his mind made up that he must resolve it one way or the other and stick with the decision. The fact that it would be difficult to explain why he had delayed acting until the following day was another factor which counted against informing the police, he reflected. On the other hand, it crossed his mind that if Hanson were caught he would probably get roped into things anyway. As for Sophie, it occurred to Phil that her troubles would not disappear simply because he had decided against doing anything: indeed, he might even be doing her a favour in the long run, by bringing the matter to a conclusion.

In his mind's eye Phil recalled the moment the previous day when he had sensed the possibility that Hanson might turn the gun on him. It was this image that prompted the thought that finally enabled him to come to a conclusion: Lucky Hanson, the man he had liked at first, and who had been good company on the golf course, was actually a maniac who would stop at nothing in order to look after his own interests. What else might he do and whom else might he harm in the process? What if Sophie proved unable to come to terms with her ordeal and started to talk to other people about what had happened? Would she be his next victim?

Phil stood up and walked purposefully towards the men's changing room. He had made a decision now, and he was certain it was the right one. His next step would be to pay a visit to Horsham police station.

'Tell me where we're going,' William demanded to know, his wrath aggravated by the fact that Lucky had already ignored two attempts to obtain this information.

'Shut up, will you? I'm trying to concentrate,' Lucky snarled, without taking his eyes off the road. He was hoping to catch up with the taxi on the way to the gym. If he could get ahead of it, he might be able to reach Jock and stop him from doing the business before Sophie could get anywhere near the place.

'I want to know why Sophie's in danger?' William persisted.

Lucky did not answer. He was trying to somehow keep William in the dark as to what was going on. He figured that if he could prevent Phil's death he might be able to persuade Sophie to keep quiet about the previous day's events. Perhaps he could go back to the original plan of paying Phil off instead. If William knew anything, there would be yet another problem to be got round. But how could he prevent him from finding out now, Lucky wondered? It crossed his mind to stop and try to lose William, but he didn't dare waste the time, and in any case he would still have to come up with an explanation later on.

They were getting close to the gym now and there was no sign of the taxi. William was fuming silently, desperate to know what was happening, but reluctant to press Lucky more forcefully and detract from his efforts to reach Sophie. Realising he might need William's assistance once they arrived, Lucky conceded he would have to give him some idea what to expect.

'Somebody's trying to kill Phil,' he began, without turning his head towards William. 'They've booby-trapped his car while he's at the gym. Sophie knows and she's trying to save him. When we get there, we've got to find her and get her away from the car.'

William's horrified stare was not apparent to Lucky, whose focus remained firmly on the road ahead. Somehow, as William gazed transfixed at Lucky, he found that he was able to discern something more from the older man's expression. William was sure that Lucky was not telling him everything. In some inexplicable way he was responsible for bringing about the situation which had placed his daughter in danger. Lucky Hanson had the look of a man who was keeping a guilty secret.

'This is your doing,' William asserted slowly, a note of contempt sounding in his voice. 'Isn't it?' he growled.

There was no reply – no futile attempt at a denial.

William shook his head as he continued:

'You...you...'

At first he could not think of a suitable word of condemnation. Then William drew the same conclusion that Phil had come to minutes earlier, and so reiterated the accusation of the driver of the taxi from which Sophie was now alighting. This time, however, the rebuke was uttered in a low, steady, deliberate voice: 'You...bloody...maniac.'

Chapter 26

It was a mistake, reflected Bruce Cartwright, to have gone along with Bennie's insistence that he could take out Hanson on his own, leaving him to take care of Follett. They should have done the job together, as they had with Burkin. His brother had been too keen to take advantage of the fact that the terminal cancer from which he was suffering had gone into remission. Everything had gone according to plan up until then. On learning of his condition, Bennie had vowed to use the time left available to him to settle old scores. He had persuaded Bruce to help him and they had agreed on the list of victims: the doctor whose refusal to treat them had left them vulnerable to disease, the man they held responsible for their sister's death, and the two men whose acts of betrayal had deprived them of their freedom.

Having disposed of Follett the previous afternoon, Bruce had made numerous attempts to get through to his brother on his mobile phone to check that all had gone smoothly his end. Unable to make contact, Bruce had set out to find him. His progress had been impaired by the fact that the Yorkshire police had set up roadblocks in an effort to catch him. He had been forced to abandon his car, flee on foot through the moors and steal another vehicle once he was in the clear. Arriving in Sussex early in the morning, Bruce had followed the route they had expected Hanson to take on his way back from the clinic. He had located the Vulcan his brother had been using for the job. The absence of any trace of Bennie added weight to his fears that something had gone badly wrong. Concluding that there was only one way to find out, Bruce had set out to complete the journey to the intended victim's home. Cartwright's research had alerted him to the fact that *Paradise* had a sophisticated security system, and as he stopped his car around the bend just short of the main entrance to the estate he was still contemplating exactly what he was going to do to gain access.

The scene which greeted him as he walked around the final corner puzzled Bruce. He could see no reason why a car had been abandoned right between the gates, its engine still running and the door on the driver's side wide open. Cartwright guessed correctly that the fact that the vehicle's presence had prevented the gates from closing would enable him to walk into the estate without triggering an alarm. Taking his gun from its holster, he made his way stealthily up the drive towards the mansion. Seeing the open front door as further evidence that someone had left, or tried to leave, in a hurry, Bruce felt renewed hope that his brother was in some way connected with this setting and had not in fact come to any harm. As he approached the mansion, he decided to try making contact one more time before he checked inside.

Stepping into the cover of the trees which bordered one side of the drive, Cartwright took out his mobile phone and called his brother's number. As he waited for a response he felt sure he could hear a tune playing. It stopped as the ringing in his ear ceased and his brother's voicemail message took over. Cartwright dialled again, this time keeping the handset away from his ear so that he could hear more clearly. Now he was certain. He stepped back onto the drive. Before the tones finished he had established that the tune was coming from the direction of the row of seven garages. He ran towards them. One further call enabled him to identify the particular garage from which the *Grande Valse* was emanating.

'Bennie!' he called out, throwing caution to the wind. Alarmed by the silence, Cartwright determined to get inside the garage. He soon deduced that the doors had to be opened from within the mansion. Brandishing his gun in front of him, he ran towards the entrance, up the steps and in through the open door.

It did not prove difficult to work out which switch on the wall opened the door. As Bruce hurried back to the garage area he once again feared the worst. The foul smell coming from within the garage which housed the Ultramobile left him in no doubt what to expect. Nevertheless he had to see for himself, to make absolutely sure of his brother's fate. It was obvious that the stench was strongest towards the rear of the vehicle. Lucky had left the sports car unlocked and Bruce soon established the whereabouts of the catch which gave him access to the boot.

Returning to the fresher air outside the garage Cartwright allowed himself a few moments of grief for his brother before turning his attention to what to do. Somehow he was sure that Hanson was not inside the mansion and he no longer had the inclination to try to track him down. For a few minutes, Bruce sat down by the open garage door and considered the situation. Then he pulled out his mobile phone again and dialled 999. Unlike Sophie earlier, he was quickly put through to the police. He told them he was ringing to report finding a body and he gave the address: *Paradise*, Copsale Road, near Maplehurst.

Bruce waited where he was until he could hear the sound of the approaching sirens. Then, closing his eyes, he tried to remember the peaceful look on the face of his sister Sarah when he discovered her body following the overdose she had taken all those years ago. Raising his gun aloft, he opened his mouth and pointed the barrel inside. For a few seconds he hesitated. Then he slowly pulled the trigger.

Chapter 27

'What sort of car are we looking for?' William asked, as Lucky sped towards the entrance to the gym. It was the first time either man had spoken since William had accused Lucky of being a maniac.

'It's a white Toyota estate,' Lucky replied. As the MG entered the complex William prayed that they would be in time. He had never been more conscious of his love for Sophie than he was at that moment. Lucky hurtled up the drive towards the gym and screeched to a halt close to the main entrance to the building. 'Oh God, please don't let Sophie come to any harm. Take me if you must, but not her,' William said to himself as both men got out of the sports car. There was no sign of Sophie, or of Phil's car, among the vehicles parked to the front of the gym. They could see that there was more parking space either side of the building and also at the rear.

'You take that side, I'll take this one,' William asserted; without waiting for an acknowledgment he sprinted towards the corner of the building. A moment later Lucky started to run in the opposite direction.

Jock could hardly believe his eyes as he surveyed the car park from the woods behind the gym. How could Sophie have possibly known what was going on? It didn't matter; she had found out somehow. As he watched her through the binoculars trying to make up her mind which of the two white Toyotas she had come across to the rear of the gym belonged to Phil he could see the look of trepidation on her face. He reasoned that since she knew what was going on she must be aware of his involvement in it. He was going to have to go on the run, he concluded. He cursed the fact that he had not brought a gun with him; he would have stood a good chance of hitting her from here. He wondered whether to risk going home to collect some things before the police came for him, but decided he would wait and see what happened here first. The fact that

Sophie was on her own meant that she may not even have reported the matter to the police yet. Maybe he would get a lucky break: perhaps Sophie would urge Phil not to inform the police in order to protect her father. Or better still, they might choose to examine the car – if one of them opened the door the blast might take them both out. So he stayed where he was and kept his binoculars trained on the gym.

Still uncertain as to which of the two seemingly identical vehicles was Phil's, Sophie decided to position herself in the middle of them. Both cars were parked in the row nearest the back of the building, one close to one end, the other right on the other end. There was no point going inside to find Phil. If she missed him and he came out before her it could be disastrous. From where she was standing, on the path that ran along the back wall of the gym, she could see if he came out, and she would also be able to prevent anyone else from getting too close to either vehicle. She concluded that she had the situation under control and breathed a sigh of relief.

'Sophie!' came a shout from behind her. Turning, she saw William running along the path towards her, passing the white Toyota near the end of the row before she had time to call to him. In a few seconds he was upon her, holding her tightly against him, kissing the side of her head, panting heavily as a result of the sprint he had put on.

As the couple held each other firmly William looked over Sophie's shoulder. He noticed a man who had come out of the back door of the gym walking in the opposite direction. It was only when the man turned sideways on as he reached the vehicle at the end of the row that he recognised him.

Looking slightly upwards at William, Sophie suddenly saw his expression change. As she looked round, William cried out: 'Phil!'

He looked in their direction just as he opened the car door. At the same time Lucky rounded the corner and realised that he was only a few feet away from Phil. There was just time for the two men to catch each other's eyes before the short delay on the booby-trap expired. Then there was a sharp flash and a loud bang: Phil was blasted into the air and Lucky was thrown against the wall of the gym.

William let go of Sophie and ran towards the burning car. Sophie stood petrified for perhaps half a minute; then she began to walk slowly, fearfully, towards the scene. The noise of the explosion drew staff and customers out of the gym, and by the time Sophie arrived there were a dozen people between her and the bodies. Before she could find her way through them, William emerged from among the crowd, took her by the arm and led her away, back in the direction from which she had come, and on round to the side of the building. As on the dreadful night of the dinner party, there was no need to say anything: his silence was all that was needed to convey the message that her father and Phil were both dead.

Jock allowed the binoculars to drop around his neck, and with a shake of his head began to pick his way back through the trees to where he had left his car. He couldn't afford to take the chance on going home. He would have to go to ground immediately and he would have to write off his half million pounds. Too bad about Lucky, as well, he reflected. After all, they went back a long way. Lucky was about the closest thing he had to a friend.

As William stood holding Sophie in his arms, a policeman approached them. He looked curiously at them for a moment, before recognising the couple as witnesses to the massacre at the Burkins.

'Excuse me, sir, I understand you saw what happened.'

William waved his hand to indicate that there was no way Sophie was ready for any questions. Half an hour had elapsed since the explosion and she had not uttered a single word. She had been crying in a way few adults ever cry, wailing like a crippled animal as she buried her head under William's chin. There were tears running down William's cheeks too. He wept for the day when Andrew Hanson finally ran out of luck, for the way in which his desire to live indefinitely had been foiled by the weakness of his character, and for the two young lives which would remain inextricably entwined as a result of a series of events for which others were responsible.

The detective waited nearby for the moment when Sophie would recover sufficiently to answer his questions. As he stood with his arms crossed in front of him another officer alighted from a nearby police car. He had received a message which he needed to pass on to his superior.

'Excuse me, sir, the superintendent says that as soon as you've finished here he wants you to go over to Maplehurst. Another murder case, by the sound of it.' He handed the senior officer a piece of paper. 'This is where you need to go,' he added.

The detective raised his eyebrows as he recalled the association between the address on the note and the young lady in front of him. He decided he could wait no longer.

'Excuse me, miss,' he began, stepping closer to the two young people.

After a few moments Sophie gradually raised her head and pointed an expressionless face in the direction of the detective.

'There's been another incident in a place called *Paradise*. You wouldn't happen to know anything about that, would you?'

Another pause followed. William stared at the policeman, bewildered, before turning to see what the response would be. At last Sophie tried to speak, but her throat did not manage to produce any sound. Eventually she somehow found the ability to slowly nod her head.